POLLYANNA'S WESTERN ADVENTURE

THE SIXTH GLAD BOOK
(Trade Mark)

POLLYANNA'S

(Trade Mark)

WESTERN
ADVENTURE

BY

HARRIET LUMMIS SMITH

GROSSET & DUNLAP

Publishers   NEW YORK

CONTENTS

POLLYANNA'S WESTERN ADVENTURE

CHAPTER I

WHEN A MAN CAN'T SLEEP

It is an exploded theory that sound sleep is proof positive of a conscience at peace, but half teasingly and half in earnest, Pollyanna frequently assured Jimmy that only a man with a spotless record could sleep as he did. Like all mothers, Pollyanna herself was roused by the least sound in the children's room. If Junior coughed hoarsely, or Judy whimpered over a bad dream, or Ruth uttered one of those inopportune calls for a "drink," by which the best trained children love to demonstrate their authority, Pollyanna was out of bed so quickly as to give ground for the suspicion that she had been lying awake, waiting for the summons. But the chances were ten to one that Jimmy would not rouse till she

1

crawled back into bed again, chilled and shivery and distressingly wide awake. Sometimes—not always, by any means—he would stir and mumble drowsily, "Kiddies wake you, dear? Why didn't you call me?" But before Pollyanna could finish telling him how glad she was that he had not been disturbed, he was off again, his deep, regular breathing proving the needlessness of her reassurance. At such times Pollyanna, smiling to herself in the dark, felt as if she were the mother of four children, with Jimmy the oldest son.

After a dozen years of taking Jimmy's capacity for sound sleep for granted, it was a shock to Pollyanna to find he had fallen into the habit of lying awake. Again and again she roused sharply, as she did when one of the children coughed or cried out, and was instantly aware that Jimmy, too, was wide awake. "Aren't you sleeping, dear?" she would ask, astonished. And he would answer carelessly, "Why, not just at this minute." But as she lay listening for the rhythmic breathing of deep slumber, so impossible to counterfeit, she became aware that the motionless figure beside her was not relaxed, but rigid; that Jimmy was keeping quiet by an effort of the will. And with this realization, Pollyanna felt a chill at her heart.

She waited for him to explain of his own accord.

Pollyanna disapproved of those women who assume that they have a right to every dollar of a husband's income, and an equal right to every thought in his head. But in this case she realized the necessity of clearing up the situation. It would not do for Jimmy to shut her out of a secret that was keeping him awake nights.

One evening when the children were asleep and Jimmy had been reading her a chapter out of one of those books rather unusual in modern fiction, planned to make the reader smile, rather than sigh, Pollyanna suddenly knew that the psychological moment had arrived. She did not give herself time to lose courage. "Jimmy," she blurted out, "why aren't you sleeping?"

"Why, because you're so entertaining, I suppose. It would be a poor return to go to sleep in the middle of it."

"No, Jimmy, I'm not joking. You were awake an endless time last night. I heard the clock strike three times before you dropped off."

"Sounds as if you were lying awake yourself." There was something sharp under the pleasantness of Jimmy's voice. "Perhaps you've got a dark secret to confide to me."

Pollyanna laid down the stocking she was darning. There was no mistaking the undercurrent of

irritation in Jimmy's tone. She was increasingly
aware that she must get to the bottom of this mystery, whatever it might be.

"Jimmy, aren't you well?" The question had a
more desperate sound than she had intended, but it
had just occurred to her that after talking of taking
out more life insurance, Jimmy had suddenly
dropped the subject. Suppose he had tried, and the
doctors had not passed him. Suppose they had told
him that his heart was in bad shape. With such a
secret to keep, of course he couldn't sleep.

"Never was better in my life," Jimmy declared
crisply. "For the Lord's sake, Pollyanna, don't
start fussing."

"Is anything wrong at the office?"

"Listen to me, my dear. I've always regarded you
as the most sensible woman of my acquaintance.
Believe it or not, that was one reason why I fell in
love with you. Now don't blast the reputation of a
life-time by an evening's folly."

Pollyanna looked at him hard. "It *is* the office,
then. Have they promoted somebody over your
head?"

"You little goose!" He laughed as if really
amused by the suggestion. "Of course not."

"Then what *have* they done?"

"Well, I suppose I'm not to have any peace until

I've explained the matter to you satisfactorily."
Jimmy spoke loudly, almost angrily, but Pollyanna's nicely trained ear discerned an intonation
indicating that his annoyance was all a sham. A
minute before he had masked real irritation under
a pretext of nonchalance. Now it was the anger
that was counterfeited. Pollyanna was certain he
found it a relief to feel he must explain.

"Well, if you must have it, they want me to take
a job I'm not interested in. They picked me out
for it in the first place, but I said no, and they put
Kendall in it. But he's not going to be equal to it.
He's sick of it and they're sick of him. And now
they're at me again."

"Why do you keep saying no?"

"Well, it's building a dam out West, one of those
jobs that can't be finished in a summer. It will take
another two years anyway. And in that time, if
luck was with me, I'd see you a few weeks altogether. Life isn't long enough for that sort of
thing. Of course, I want to get ahead, just as any
fellow would, but the idea of coming back home,
two years from now, and getting acquainted with
my children all over again doesn't appeal to me."

"But why can't we go with you?" Pollyanna cried,
wondering that this obvious solution had not occurred to him.

"Impossible, dear. You see," explained Jimmy gently, "it's a regular wilderness, miles from a railroad, without schools or any of the conveniences of life. You'd feel as if you'd gone back several centuries. Roughing it is all very well for a few weeks, but not for two years on end. I told them it was out of the question when they first offered me the job, but now they're insisting on my taking time to consider it."

"They think it's a great chance, then?"

"Well, I suppose it would be an opening wedge," Jimmy answered carelessly. "But as I say, it's out of the question for a family man, and there's no use talking."

"Wait, Jimmy. If your chance has come, you're going to take it. As for roughing it, I don't know why I shouldn't as well as any other woman. One of my great-grandmothers—I've forgotten how many *greats,* but a lot of them—came over to America in the seventeenth century from a nice, comfortable home in Devonshire, and roughed it in earnest. She had the Indians to dread besides all the rest. If I thought there was any danger that the children would be scalped, I wouldn't go. But just because there aren't any bath-tubs or running water or—"

"Very likely no water in the house at all," Jimmy interrupted. "Everything to be carried from a spring somewhere. And what about the children's education?"

Pollyanna did a little thinking.

"Would they pay you well, Jimmy?"

"Pretty fair." Jimmy's tone was painstakingly off-hand, but something revealed to his sympathetic listener his real estimate of the salary he belittled.

"Then why can't we have a governess for the children? She'd be company for me when you were away. And I could help her a little. You know I'm a pretty fair French and German scholar. At least I ought to be, after all the years I spent abroad."

"You'd never find anyone willing to go to such a place—at least not anyone you'd be willing to take."

"I'm not so sure of that. Lots of girls have an adventurous streak in them, and would like to try something different. I don't say we'd find the right person right away, but I'm sure there's somebody, somewhere, who'd just jump at the chance. When do we start?"

"When do we start?" Jimmy repeated. "Oh, it's all settled, is it? My opinion doesn't count." But while he mocked, his eyes were alight with tenderness, and he captured one of the hands, again busy with the mending, and held it a willing prisoner. "You're a good scout, Pollyanna," he said, avoiding

with modern self-consciousness the more revealing
terms his ancestors would have used under like circumstances. "It's lucky you haven't got a husband
who would encourage you in your morbid passion
for self-sacrifice."

"What's good for you, Jimmy, is good for us
all," said Pollyanna. "We want to give the children
all the advantages we can, and to do that, you'll have
to take every chance that is offered you. You can't
make bricks without straw any more than anyone
else." She attacked the big hole in Junior's stocking with an air of intense concentration, but in reality her thoughts were circumnavigating the globe.
They flew, swifter than light, to a new home in what
Jimmy had called the wilderness, its outlines so
vague in her own mind that she could not have said
whether it most resembled the log cabin of the
pioneers, or an Indian tepee. They darted to Aunt
Polly, spending the winter at Nice, and writing home
enthusiastic letters. She thought of the friends to
whom she would soon be saying good-by, and of
the new friends she would soon be making. She
thought rather anxiously of Nancy, so proud of the
new electric refrigerator and the latest electric
sweeper. Was it really fair to ask Nancy to turn
pioneer with them? There were, of course, plenty
of people who would be overjoyed to secure her

services. She could get a dozen places without going six blocks in any direction. Nancy must be made to understand just what she would sacrifice if she cast her fortunes with them.

"I think we might as well rent the house furnished," remarked Pollyanna, as casually as if she had been a real estate agent. "It wouldn't pay to move the furniture out there and back."

"Out where? Oh, are you still harping on that crazy notion?" Jimmy grinned at her over the top of the book he was pretending to read, not noticing that he held it upside down. There was a look in his eyes as if he wanted to hug her. Pollyanna shook her head over the obtuseness of the best of men. He had lived with her twelve years, without knowing that she was ready to follow him to the world's end. He was really surprised by her determination to make him accept the opportunity which intuition told her would prove a turning-point in his career.

Pollyanna resolved not to discuss the prospective upheaval with any of her friends till the matter was actually settled, a decision which rendered Jimmy uneasy. "Have you asked Aunt Ruth what she thought of this scheme?" he inquired one day.

"No," said Pollyanna. After a pause she added, "And what's more, I'm not going to."

"She'll think it rather queer, won't she, if all at once we spring the news that we're going to turn our backs on civilization? She won't understand why we haven't spoken of it."

"It's our own affair, Jimmy. And we know so well what we ought to do that there's no point in asking advice. It would only complicate matters." Thanks to Pollyanna's vivid imagination, she could in fancy see Mrs. Pendleton's face when the plan was laid before her, and hear her horrified exclamations. Dear Aunt Ruth had been so enfolded in luxury all her life that she had come to think of it as essential, in the same category as sunshine and fresh air. But Pollyanna reminded herself that even bath tubs were quite a recent innovation. Many generations had lived comfortably without electric lights or telephones. Millions still dispensed with these luxuries without any sense of deprivation. The only essential to her happiness, Pollyanna was sure, was that they should all be together.

Nancy was the only person she took into her confidence. In her determination not to mislead Nancy, she painted the picture of their future home in such dark colors that if Jimmy had heard her, he would have vetoed the plan on the spot.

"You see, Nancy, it'll be a good deal like camping out summer and winter, too. We won't have a nice house as we do here. Everything will be rough and we'll have to put up with lots of things that won't please us, and do without lots of others we've always been used to. Probably there won't be any stores for miles and miles, and we'll run short of coffee and butter and have to use makeshifts. And as likely as not, we'll have to carry all the water we use from a well outside the house."

A sniff from Nancy put a period to Pollyanna's eloquence. She became aware that Nancy was sitting with her chin tilted.

"I know I ain't so young as I uster be, but I guess I can hold my own with most of the modern young fry. But if you'd ruther have somebody lighter on her feet, Miss Pollyanna, jest say so right out plain. I'm not one for beatin' 'round the bush, I ain't, I ain't."

"Nancy! You darling, silly old Nancy! I could shake you. Don't you know it would almost kill me to lose you, that I'd feel as if the bottom had dropped out of everything? But when I know you could have a comfortable home and good wages, it just doesn't seem fair to carry you off into the wilderness—"

Pollyanna astonished herself by bursting into tears. It was anything but premeditated. She was not one of the women who can weep at will, drowning out all opposition by timely showers. But she had been under a strain ever since the discovery that Jimmy was not sleeping well, and Nature, catching her off her guard, pulled a safety valve and relieved her taut nerves.

Nancy was overwhelmed by contrition. "Now, my lamb, I've gone and made you cry. Guess I'm gettin' to be a cantankerous old woman."

"No—nothing of the sort," sobbed Pollyanna. "I'm just fo-foolish, that's all." She beamed at Nancy through her tears, her smile irradiating her wet eyes till Nancy thought of rainbows. "I don't know why I'm crying unless it's because I'm gl-glad you won't leave us."

Nancy compressed her lips. "Miss Pollyanna, you can't get rid o' me, an' you'd better not try. If you was poor, I'd work for nothin' an' be glad of the chance, I would, I would."

Having sworn Nancy to secrecy, Pollyanna kept her own counsel till Jimmy had come to a definite understanding with his firm. And then when she broke the startling news to her family and friends, she congratulated herself that she had not done it earlier. It was not necessary to devise answers to their arguments, because discussing the matter was a mere waste of breath. For better or for worse, the thing was settled.

"I can't imagine what Jimmy is thinking of," cried Aunt Ruth, her Boston culture temporarily obscured by a delightfully human fit of temper. "Dragging you and the children off into the wilds."

"He's not dragging us, Aunt Ruth. I insisted on his going and refused to be left behind."

"I'm ashamed of you both," Aunt Ruth scolded. "You should think of the children, if not of yourselves. It will upset their schooling, and they were getting on so nicely."

"We're planning to have a governess. And besides, I'm sure they are going to learn lots of useful things that aren't taught in schools."

"Suppose one of the children were taken ill."

Pollyanna winced. The same question had waked her out of a sound sleep more than once recently. She answered Aunt Ruth as she had answered her own forebodings. "There must be doctors to be had."

"Country doctors," commented Aunt Ruth witheringly.

"It's been a year or over since there has been a doctor in this house. Out there the children won't be exposed to contagious diseases as they are here. They'll be out of doors a lot and I expect to bring them home even healthier than they are now."

"And I expect to see you come back a broken-

down, middle-aged woman," prophesied Aunt Ruth
cheerfully. "There's no mystery about the fact that
our great-grandmothers were old women at forty.
Hard work did it, the same thing you're choosing
for yourself. The idea of a rational woman's turning her back on all the comforts of life—"

"That's what our pioneer ancestors did, the ones
we're so awfully proud of," Pollyanna interrupted
pertly, and Aunt Ruth's eloquence evaporated in a
gasp. She was an ardent D. A. R. worker, and extravagantly proud of the fact that her ancestors were
settled in New England a hundred years before the
Declaration of Independence was thought of. And
while she replied stiffly that times had changed,
Pollyanna congratulated herself on having used the
one argument which would silence her reproachful
relative, even if it did not convince her.

CHAPTER II

PACKING

POLLYANNA was packing. There were trunks all over the house, and each one looked big enough to carry the personal belongings of her entire family. But when it came to the test, they proved inadequate. Certain things she had confidently expected to take along had to be set aside, either to be stored or sent by mail.

The children complicated matters by bringing her their treasures by the armful. They dumped them beside the trunks,—electric trains, doll houses, Teddy bears, building blocks, dolls of every size and description, tea-sets, games. Junior, who had recently acquired bookish tastes, appeared carrying a zigzag, teetery column of books which began as far down as his short arms could reach, and terminated at his chin.

"Mother, I guess you've forgotten these."

"Oh, Junior, we've sent on such a big box of books, I'm afraid I can't take any more."

"But I can't be separated from Peter, Mother. We're—we're chums."

15

Pollyanna sighed. If Peter had been the hero of a single volume, it would not have been so serious, but his adventures ran through a long series. And yet there was an earnestness in Junior's voice that stirred her sympathies. To him Peter was a living boy, an actual chum. There were so many friends he must leave, it seemed a pity not to let Peter accompany him. "Put them down on the floor," she said weakly. "I'll see what I can do."

It was equally trying when Ruth staggered into the room, Jiggs under one arm, Sin under the other. The bodies of both pets hung limp. They would have resented such treatment from an older person, and expressed that resentment in no uncertain terms, but like most animals, they made allowances for children.

"Muvver," panted Ruth, "what trunk is Jiggs going in?"

"Put Jiggs down, dear, and Sin, too. Pets don't travel in trunks." It was illogical but Pollyanna felt guilty. While she had told the truth, it was by no means the whole truth. For after long considera-tion she and Jimmy had reached the conclusion that Jiggs was not suited for the life of the frontier. His impudence demanded an urban setting. Jiggs was perfectly capable of charging a grizzly bear in a moment of excitement. And while Pollyanna was not anticipating the proximity of grizzly bears in her new abode, she felt that Jiggs would complicate the experiment unnecessarily.

A family named Hemingway were to rent the house furnished, and they had agreed to keep Sin. They liked cats, and Sin impressed them as an exemplary specimen of his tribe. But they had their doubts about dogs, and Jiggs confirmed this uncertainty by misbehaving each time they came to the house. He barked at them from the moment they entered till they took their departure. Of course he was turned out of doors at the first indication of misconduct, but he merely stationed himself under the bay window, and barked continuously, shrilly, and insultingly. Vexed as Pollyanna was, she was impressed by the insight such atrocious behavior indicated. In some uncanny fashion, Jiggs had discovered that these strangers had designs on his home. He had never acted that way before. Pollyanna said as much, but apparently it did not advance Jiggs in the good graces of her prospective tenants to learn that he had singled them out of all the world to treat with contumely.

Sin, on the other hand, was evidently trying to make a good impression. He did not always respond to the advances of strangers, but to the Hemingways, he was affability itself. He arched his back.

He purred. When by these amenities he had
attracted the attention of the future occupants of the
house, he rolled over and lay on his back, holding
his paws in the drooping attitude of supplication.
The Hemingways were delighted.

Sadie saved the situation by offering to take Jiggs.
Jamie Junior wanted a dog and Jiggs was accustomed to children. It seemed an ideal solution of
the problem, but Pollyanna put off informing her
own children that Jiggs was not to accompany them.
She was not quite sure that she could tell the news
without weeping.

Everything had turned out in a way to justify
Pollyanna's optimism. The tenants were friends of
the McGills, just the sort of people, Anne McGill
said, you'd like to have using your things. Of
course, Pollyanna realized ruefully that there *were*
no such people. It gave her a sick feeling, like
jealousy, to picture Mr. Hemingway occupying the
chair sacred to Jimmy, or Mrs. Hemingway turning
the nursery into a sewing-room, as she had
announced her intention of doing. But she admitted
that some people were preferable to others when it
was a question of using your belongings, and that
the Hemingways were as little objectionable as any
tenants could be.

Jimmy had been gone a month already. In a

region destitute of hotels, it was necessary for him to find a dwelling-place and render it habitable before the family arrived. He had been there two weeks, when he telegraphed Pollyanna of his success in securing a house, but the description contained in his next letter was not altogether reassuring.

The house was old, the adobe walls two feet in thickness, promising warmth in winter and coolness in summer, Jimmy explained. There were three rooms on the ground floor, and two above, not counting the kitchen which was a wooden lean-to. The house did not have water, but there was a pump in the yard, not more than twenty feet from the back door. The cellar, instead of being under the house, was a dug-out convenient to the pump, a fair-sized room, Jimmy explained, hollowed out of the side of the hill, and furnished with a wooden door. Vegetables could be kept safely in these cellars all winter, even in the severest weather, Jimmy said, evidently quoting from his new landlord.

"The scarcity of bedrooms may worry you," Jimmy wrote, "but if you use one of the downstairs rooms as a bedroom, that makes three, which is excessive for this part of the country, for all that large families are fashionable. A porch runs along the front of the house and down one side, and we

can use it as a sleeping porch if we want to. There
are several good fireplaces, but I've ordered a stove
for the living-room, to use in the coldest weather.
Around here, they burn wood mostly, though we can
buy coal at the mines if we send for it, and load it
ourselves."

One of the real disappointments was that the
house was some dozen miles from the scene of
Jimmy's labors. Pollyanna had fancied him coming
home for luncheon, and now, she realized unhappily,
he would not always be home for dinner. But the
men engaged in the construction work were a rough
lot, many of them unable to speak English, and
Jimmy preferred to locate his family at a reasonable
distance.

"It's a wonderful country," Jimmy wrote, "and a
wonderful climate. I feel like another man already,
and I have a picture of you getting younger and
younger, so that when we go back to Massachusetts,
our friends will tell you how young you've grown,
thinking you must be Judy."

Pollyanna chuckled over the optimistic prophecy,
recalling how Aunt Ruth, not so optimistic, had
assured her that she would return prematurely
middle-aged. The cellar and the pump backed up
Aunt Ruth, but the bracing climate was on Jimmy's
side. "Anyway I shan't try to do the impossible."

Pollyanna promised herself. "And I mean to get as much fun out of it as I can."

The selection of a governess proved a problem. In answer to Pollyanna's discreet advertisements, many applicants presented themselves, most of them middle-aged, and some elderly. After Pollyanna had explained the situation in detail, their answers showed that they had not grasped a thing she had been saying, as, for example, when one of them stipulated that she should be given forty-eight hours to herself every other week.

"But what would you do with it?" asked Pollyanna, purely out of curiosity, for she had felt from the start that this nervous, frail-looking spinster would not meet her requirements.

"Why, I'd run into town, shop, go to the theatre, possibly, or to a concert—"

"Yes, I thought you had something like that in mind," said Pollyanna, "but you see there *is* no town."

"No town?"

"None near enough to be available, and no shops, and, of course, no theatres."

"But I shouldn't think of accepting such a position!" the woman exclaimed almost shrilly. "I should go crazy, penned up with a crowd of children. It would be worse than penal servitude."

Pollyanna suppressed a sharp answer. After all the woman's attitude did not justify her in losing her temper. Mothers, it was true, did not consider insanity an inevitable sequel of spending all their time with their children, but there was a reason for that. She looked at the twitching, querulous face with sudden sympathy. Teaching children without loving children must be the hardest sort of hard work.

She was getting very anxious because of her failure to find a satisfactory governess, when the right one appeared. At least Pollyanna felt from the start that she would prove the right one. She was young, though not, of course, as young as she looked. With her slender figure and bobbed hair, she might easily have passed for sixteen, but it seemed she was a college graduate, with over a year's experience as a substitute teacher in the public schools.

"I don't like teaching a bit," she told Pollyanna, "and yet it's the thing I've been fitting myself for all my life. When I saw your advertisement, I felt like Alice when she got the little gold key that unlocked the door into the garden."

The reference to Alice in Wonderland was a bond of sympathy. Pollyanna had to remind herself that familiarity with her favorite heroine, though important, was not the sole qualification necessary in a governess.

"If you don't like to teach," she said, a worried frown creasing her smooth forehead, "I'm afraid you wouldn't enjoy this position. It's teaching we want you for."

"Of course," said the girl. "But you see, I like teaching itself. And I adore children. It's the records that are so loathsome, and the report cards, and having a form for everything."

"Oh!" breathed Pollyanna, and felt encouraged.

"Everything nowadays has to be reduced to a formula," Miss Blythe explained, "children and all. And then everything has to be recorded. Teaching seems to be more bookkeeping than anything else."

Pollyanna felt sure that report cards could be eliminated in a home school. Though hopeful, she was cautious. Her circumstances would not be regarded as ideal for entertaining a stranger, but disregarding this, she promptly invited Miss Blythe to come out the following day and spend the weekend as her guest.

The girl's face crinkled delightedly. "Want to look me over and see if I'll do?"

"You might like to look us over, too. It's a sort of 'for better or for worse' arrangement, and we don't want to make a mistake."

"All right. I'll come. But I don't see," said Miss Blythe with that saucy smile of hers, "that it will help you much. I'm bound to be on my good behavior."

"No, you'll be the one to benefit," laughed Pollyanna, "for a stranger in the house invariably means that the children are on their worst behavior."

The experiment told her just what she wanted to know. Miss Blythe had a faculty with children. She won their confidence without appearing to seek it. She did not patronize them, after the fashion of the professional child-lover, with pretended enthusiasms and saccharine endearments. She erred on the side of brusqueness, if anything, and Pollyanna suspected this was due to fear of pretending what she did not feel, in order to win favor. From her observation of the girl, Pollyanna gained a pleasing impression of sincerity, kindliness and a genuine sympathy for a child's point of view. Moreover Miss Blythe was really intelligent, and to her prospective employer this counted largely in her favor.

Late in the afternoon, they compared notes. "I hope," said Pollyanna, "you liked us well enough so a year or two in our society won't seem impossible."

Miss Blythe had dropped into one of the children's little rocking-chairs. Her elbows on her knees, her chin resting on her cupped hands, she looked startlingly juvenile.

"I'm crazy to go with you, Mrs. Pendleton," she

said. "I was born and brought up in this state. I've been to Niagara Falls, and to Washington, and that's the extent of my travels. I want something as different as can be. I'd rather see a cowboy than a king. If you take me, I'll make you think it was the best day's work you ever did."

Pollyanna laughed. She liked the audacity of the speech, its youthful extravagance. She liked Dorothy Blythe, and though, as a matter of form, she planned to consult the references the girl had given her, she had practically made up her mind. After the inflexible females who had interviewed her regarding this position, Dorothy seemed too good to be true. "Could you be ready to start in about a week?" she asked.

"I could be ready to start in a day. I'd start in an hour, if that was the only way to get the position."

"Everything will be at sixes and sevens when we get there," said Pollyanna. "Mr. Pendleton bought the furniture from a mail order house, and he'll try to be ready for us after a fashion. But it will take a little time to make the place really habitable."

"It'll be fun, though, won't it?" said Dorothy, and if it had not seemed impolitic, Pollyanna would have informed her on the spot that she was engaged. She wanted a girl young enough to feel that the inevitable hardships were part of the adventure.

Miss Blythe's references were satisfactory. She had been a good student, and a successful substitute teacher. The following fall, if not before, she would have been assigned to a school. The question of a governess settled, Pollyanna felt that her most difficult problems were solved. All that was left was to decide what articles were to be taken along and what left behind, in addition to the constantly recurring puzzle, how to make a trunk already full, carry half as much again.

Several days before the time set for their departure, Pollyanna transferred Jiggs to his new home. The children were out for the afternoon, and borrowing Lorraine's car, and chauffeur, Pollyanna drove to Sadie's. Jiggs' reluctance to accompany her increased her respect for his intelligence. Jiggs, always deliriously happy if invited into an automobile, actually had to be collared and dragged inside the car. And then, instead of being alert to see what was happening on the street, he crouched in the corner of the seat, glaring at her with bulging, reproachful eyes. Even the pleasure with which the Carews welcomed their new acquisition could not free Pollyanna from the illogical impression that she had done something to be ashamed of.

Pollyanna was in for a hard day. For when she reached home, the children were back and looking anxiously for Jiggs. She made the truth as little harrowing as possible, but Junior went to his room, and locked the door, disregarding the summons to supper. Judy cried over her meal, and Ruth, the only member of the family with an appetite, attempted to console her sister by observing, "Muvver's naughty, ain't she, Judy?" And at this frank expression of opinion, Pollyanna herself was on the point of tears.

Late the next afternoon, Sadie telephoned to ask what delicacy Jiggs particularly fancied. "Raw beef," said Pollyanna promptly. "What's the matter? Won't he eat?"

"He hasn't yet. Feels a little strange, I suppose. I thought I'd tempt him with something nice."

Twenty-four hours later she telephoned again to ask what veterinary Pollyanna had employed. "I don't believe Jiggs is sick, but I'd like an expert opinion from someone who is used to the dog."

Pollyanna gave the necessary information, her heart sinking. It was Saturday, and Monday they were leaving. Of course she could not alter her plans, and cancel her reservations because a dog was ailing, but to go away leaving Jiggs sick seemed heartless. This time she cried a little and felt better.

Early the next day, Sadie called her. "Pollyanna, this dog is driving me crazy."

"Is he sick?"

"He hasn't eaten a mouthful since he came. He simply ignores us. He crawls under the couch and there he stays. But he isn't asleep, Pollyanna. If you look under, you can see his eyes shining in the dark. I believe he knows he's going to be left behind, and it's breaking his heart."

Pollyanna reached a reckless conclusion. "Then I'll have to take him along. He might as well be killed by a mountain lion as die of grief. When shall I get him?"

"We'll bring him right over," Sadie answered, "before you have a chance to change your mind I tell you, Pollyanna, I wouldn't have that dog left to die on my hands for a million dollars."

Perhaps because of this last-minute change of plans, their departure next day was a comparatively cheerful occasion. Jiggs, duly muzzled and tagged, was given in charge of a sympathetic porter. And as if he realized that acquiescence was the price of accompanying the family, he submitted meekly to being led away.

A host of Pollyanna's friends were down to see her off, so many that an inquisitive old lady inquired what was happening, and a fellow traveler sarcastically replied, "Nothin' but the Queen o' Roumania takin' another little trip." Aunt Ruth was there, her eyelids slightly reddened, and Uncle John, laden with enough books and magazines to start a circulating library. The Carews had brought Jamie Junior to say good-by to Aunt Pollyanna, and he said it at intervals of thirty seconds, for a good fifteen minutes before the train was due. Lorraine and Frank were on hand, of course, and the McGills, Philip very downcast over the prospect of losing his favorite chum. In fact so many kind friends had gathered to see Pollyanna off that it brought home to her impressively how much she was leaving behind.

The gate was opened at last. They made an imposing line as they climbed aboard the Pullman, Dorothy Blythe, Nancy, and the three children, with Pollyanna bringing up the rear. They found their sections in the centre of the coach, and Pollyanna moved quickly to the window, waving her hand and smiling down at Uncle John and Aunt Ruth who had bribed their way past the gateman. The dear, familiar faces blurred as the train trembled and began to move.

"Muvver," exclaimed the too observant Ruth, "is you cwyin'? 'Cause your eyes look funny."

Pollyanna beamed down at her. "Crying!" she repeated with the scorn such a preposterous suggestion deserved. "Why we're as glad as we can be, because we're going to see Daddy."

CHAPTER III

THE FIRST CALLER

IT was fortunate for Pollyanna that she reached her destination in the spring, that season of hopeful expectancy when the roadside path, trampled hard by innumerable feet, feels within itself the possibility of achieving beauty, and the old tree, gnarled and broken, answers the thrill of reviving life with buds and blossoms. In the spring she saw her new home not as it was, but as it might become.

The twenty-mile drive from the railway station was an ordeal, for the unpaved roads were full of ruts, and the jolting of the car made progress slow and painful. Occasionally they came to a rocky stretch where ruts were impossible, but Pollyanna preferred that discomfort to the sensation of sheer terror which assailed her when the car made its way along a narrow shelf, with a rocky wall, rising sheer and steep on one hand, while on the other, the ground fell away into a ravine hundreds of feet deep. When at length they reached their destination, she felt that they had had a series of hair-breadth escapes.

The house which was to be her home for an indefinite period was not unpicturesque, as she saw at a glance. Built of adobe, with a wide chimney at the end, it had that look of fitness which is the basis of all beauty. In the rear was the barn, unnecessarily large, since it would only be called on to house two automobiles and a cow. The wife of the ranch owner, Mrs. Schroeder, had been on hand since morning, and an agreeable odor of roasting beef met them at the door. There was a fire in the big fireplace, for they were so far above sea-level that there was a perceptible chill under the softness of the spring air.

"This is my wife, Mrs. Schroeder," Jimmy said, drawing Pollyanna toward the stout woman in the faded gingham. "You can see for yourself that she's as nice as I said."

Instead of accepting Pollyanna's extended hand, Mrs. Schroeder raised both her own above her head.

"Oh, a fine lady!" she cried disapprovingly. "You hadn't ought to 'a' done it, Mister. This here ain't no place for a fine lady."

Pollyanna's astonishment was blended with consternation. Under certain circumstances, to be called a fine lady might be regarded as a compliment, but it was so evident that Mrs. Schroeder had, at a glance, weighed her in the balance and found her wanting, that she felt it imperative to defend herself against the charge.

"Oh, Mrs. Schroeder, I'm nothing of the sort," she cried. "See, here are my children. One couldn't be a fine lady and look after three lively little folks like these, could one?"

"It ain't no place for fine ladies, this here ain't," persisted Mrs. Schroeder, stubbornly. "You hadn't ought to 'a' done it, Mister."

Pollyanna was relieved to find that Mrs. Schroeder, having expressed her disapproval of Jimmy's choice of wives, accepted the other members of the party without comment, unfavorable or otherwise. "Dinner's ready," she announced, with an air of finality, and began to dish up the potatoes, boiled in their jackets, and in such quantities that Pollyanna gasped. She hurried the children away to remove their wraps, but before they were ready, the meal was on the table, all of it, even to the pies. And though it seemed to have been planned for Brobdingnagian appetites, it was an inviting dinner, too.

"We're one place short, aren't we, Mrs. Schroeder?" Jimmy asked as the family gathered about the table. "I believe you've left yourself out."

Mrs. Schroeder sniffed. "I ain't one to set along with fine folks," she replied. "I'll be starting for home where my own work's waiting." And despite the joint protests of Jimmy and Pollyanna, she took an immediate departure.

"What Mrs. Schroeder lacks in the social graces," remarked Jimmy, beginning to carve the beef, "she makes up in her knowledge of the art of cooking. I don't know what kind of pies those are, but I'll bet a dollar to the hole in a doughnut that they're good. Nancy, why aren't you sitting down?"

"Now, Mr. Pendleton," cried Nancy bridling, "I guess I know my place."

"Come, Nancy, sit down with the rest of us," laughed Pollyanna. "I see we'll have to be careful or our neighbors will boycott us for putting on airs." Then turning to Jimmy, she asked, "Was Mrs. Schroeder living in this house when you rented it?"

"She lived here part of the time. Schroeder owns two ranches, each with a good substantial house, and they have kept both furnished after a fashion. When either one found the other's society trying, he or she moved over into this house. As far as Mrs. Schroeder goes, she's really a very nice woman, though hardly a tactful one. Nancy, what are you doing out in the kitchen? Why don't you come and eat your dinner?"

An indignant Nancy appeared in the doorway.

"Mr. Pendleton, I've worked for particular people all my life, and I ain't a-goin' to fall into loose ways, jest because we're livin' where folks don't know what's what. I know my place and I'm a-goin' to keep my place."

She stalked back into the kitchen, with the air of one whose ideas of propriety have received a severe shock, and giving up, for the time being, the attempt to conquer her prejudices, Pollyanna devoted herself to her dinner. She was astonished to find herself ravenous. The journey had seemed long and tiresome, and after the first day, the menu of the dining-car had failed to arouse her enthusiasm. Dorothy Blythe had been very helpful with the children, but had found time for an intensive flirtation with a young man on his way to the Pacific coast. They exchanged addresses as they parted, each promising to write, and Pollyanna reflected that if the journey had been longer, she might have lost her governess before she had fairly started on the work for which she had been engaged.

On the whole Jiggs had made the trip as comfortably as any of them. When Pollyanna visited the baggage car, she generally found Jiggs occupying a chair, while the man to whom it belonged sat on a trunk nearby. The train men all liked Jiggs, and when the train stopped for a few minutes, they improved the opportunity to give him a little run. And they were so ready to share their meals with him that Pollyanna realized there was serious danger of his being overfed. Jiggs was tremendously excited by his new environment, and now was running about sniffing, scratching and barking from sheer lightness of heart.

"If they consider you too fine for your surroundings," Jimmy told Pollyanna, "I don't know what they'll say to Jiggs. I've always regarded Jiggs as the aristocrat of the family."

"Well, he was popular on the train, anyway," said Pollyanna, "and if the train men liked him, I don't know why the people here shouldn't."

"As far as I've been able to learn," observed Jimmy, "very little sentiment is wasted on dogs in this part of the world. They seem to be regarded from a purely practical standpoint, in the same class with a machine, though not so valuable. Most of them are kept chained all day and are underfed, in order to make them fierce, so they're rather ugly customers. Master Jiggs had better keep his distance."

"Of course they're ugly, chained up and half-starved!" Pollyanna exclaimed, but she made a mental note of a danger to Jiggs she had not taken into account.

As Pollyanna had expected, she found the house

ready for occupancy after a fashion. The furniture had been uncrated and disposed in the appropriate rooms. The beds had been set up. Screwdrivers had been used where needed. The furniture Jimmy had purchased was of a sort one could use several years and then abandon without a regret, and though she sighed as she looked it over, she acknowledged that he had been wise in his selection. The beds were metal, painted white, like hospital cots. The living-room furniture was plain and substantial, if not beautiful. But when a few pictures were up and the books in place, everything would look very different, Pollyanna told herself. After all it was no especial triumph to make a house attractive when all the resources of the interior decorators were at your disposal. But to dispense with their aid, and yet have a home that met all the requirements, was a worthwhile victory for any woman.

So absorbed was Pollyanna in the task of getting her house in order that she found little time to question Jimmy as to the characteristics of what he disrespectfully referred to as "the natives," and even had she done so, she would hardly have been prepared for what happened a few days after her arrival. Dorothy Blythe, who had been of great assistance in the business of getting settled, had taken the children and gone for a walk. Nancy was

enjoying her usual afternoon nap in the kitchen
rocking-chair, and Pollyanna herself was re-arrang-
ing the contents of one of the bookcases, with which
she had received so much help from the children
that most of the books were standing on their heads.
Then a loud knocking at the porch door challenged
her attention, and she found herself as astonished as
Robinson Crusoe would have been if someone had
interrupted his labors by knocking on his bower. She
knew she had neighbors, using the words in a more
elastic sense than was common in New England, but
she had not expected to hear from them so soon.

When, in answer to the summons, she opened the
door, her first sensation was one of thankfulness that
the children were away. For she was too well versed
in Wild West fiction not to recognize a desperado
when she saw one. The man on the porch was the
most villainous specimen she had ever encountered.
To begin with, his eyes were crossed, and it would
have required some especial nobility of feature to
have counteracted the effect of that oblique gaze.
But none of his features was noble. His nose was
squat, his chin so covered with stubble that it was
difficult to determine its shape, and his mouth was
twisted. His skin had evidently once been fair, but
now was so freckled that he reminded the horrified
observer of some curiously spotted animal. As if

nature had not done enough to render him a terrifying object, he carried a gun.

Pollyanna, confronting this unexpected appari-
tion at her own door, suddenly felt weak in the
knees. Jiggs had accompanied the children on their
walk. There was not even a little dog to call to her
assistance. With whitening face she stared at him,
waiting for the worst.

"Boss to home?"

Pollyanna realized that the occasion called for
diplomacy. If she replied that Jimmy would not be
home for several hours, she practically acknowledged
herself at the ruffian's mercy. In a frightened pipe,
which she vainly tried to render casual, she replied,
"Not just at this minute."

The man shifted his gun, and Pollyanna resolved
that if he said "Hands up!" she would instantly
obey. She would give him whatever he wanted,
only, unfortunately, there was little in the house a
thief would care for. Their silver was plated ware.
She had practically no money, for their household
supplies were ordered by mail, and paid for by check.
As they were situated, cash was the least of their
needs. Perhaps the man was after Jimmy's clothes.
The dilapidated condition of his garments gave a
certain plausibility to the conjecture.

She waited, her heart thumping, but the man with

the gun did not order her to put up her hands. And
at length she brought herself to inquire in a shaking
voice, "Is there—any message?"

"Huh?"

"Is there anything you'd like me to tell Mr.
Pendleton?"

"I'll wait."

He sat down on one of the porch chairs, leaving
his gun within easy reach. And then a new and
more terrifying explanation for his presence flashed
into Pollyanna's mind. Perhaps his motive was
worse than robbery. Perhaps Jimmy had discharged
him, as, judging from his appearance, he had every
reason to do, and the man had come to take his
revenge.

Pollyanna closed the door softly, and stood a minute trying to make up her mind what to do. It was
more than two hours before the time Jimmy usually
arrived, though there was always a chance that he
might return early. This possibility made her feel
the need of haste. Jimmy must be warned and
warned in time.

She stole into the kitchen and roused Nancy, who
started up rubbing her eyes. "I was takin' forty
winks, Miss Pollyanna. Dinner tonight won't be—
sake's alive! What's the matter?"

"Nancy, there's a man here waiting to see Mr.

Pendleton. I don't like his looks. He's armed, and I'm afraid it means trouble."

Nancy wrung her hands. "Oh, Miss Pollyanna, why did we ever come to such a place?"

"Sh! Nancy, I want you to go out back of the house, and around through the woods, so as to get back on the road without being seen. Then wait till Mr. Pendleton comes. It may be a long time, but no matter. Tell him just what I've told you, that there's a man here waiting to see him. He's a repulsive looking man, say, with crossed eyes and a freckled skin. Tell him the man is armed. Then Mr. Pendleton will know what to do."

Nancy caught her hands. "Miss Pollyanna, *you* creep out of the house, and let *me* stay. I can't go off and leave you alone, with a critter like that. I'm an old woman," whimpered Nancy, beginning to weep. "An' it don't matter much what happens to me."

Pollyanna patted the hand clutching hers. "Hush, Nancy. I can't leave. The children will be coming. Do as I say."

After Nancy's departure, the minutes dragged. The man on the porch sat immobile as a statue, his hand on the gun leaning against his chair. After what seemed an interminable time, the voices of Dorothy Blythe and the children came to Polly-

anna's ears. She ran from the back of the house
and by warning gestures, checked their chatter before they were near enough to hear her voice. If
the man on the porch wanted revenge, here was his
chance. Something in her white face and unnatural
manner subdued the excitement of the children, and
Dorothy looked at her in perplexity.

"Come into the kitchen, children, and don't talk.
There's someone on the porch and I don't want to
disturb him."

"Is he taking a nap?" queried Ruth, much interested.

"Perhaps. Anyway, we won't disturb him."
Pollyanna gathered Jiggs into her arms and carried
him indoors. Like most dogs, Jiggs had a strong
antipathy to shabby clothing, and a man out-at-
elbows was a suspicious character in his eyes. For-
tunately Jiggs was weary. His walk had abounded
in thrills for a city-bred dog, and now he was satisfied to be treated as an infant.

In the kitchen they talked in whispers, while Pollyanna vainly tried to appear unconcerned. She made
more than one attempt to start the preparations for
the evening meal, and gave it up as a bad job. Even
the simplest tasks were impossible, while her mind
was so distraught.

Though she had waited so impatiently for the

sound of Jimmy's Ford, her heart almost stopped beating when at last her straining ears caught its familiar rattle. White-lipped she turned to Dorothy.

"Keep the children here," she said, without explanation, and went to the front of the house. She could see Jimmy turning in from the road, Nancy on the seat beside him. She had hoped that the car would be filled with men in sufficient numbers to overcome the most daring criminal, but apparently Jimmy preferred to attend to the matter himself.

Very deliberately the man arose, and picking up his gun, slouched down the steps. Pollyanna looked about her wildly. If only she had a weapon of some sort, so she could attack the miscreant in the rear. There was nothing of the sort in the house, but with the thought of distracting the man's attention and giving Jimmy a chance, she ran to the door.

The two had met before she got the door open. They were shaking hands, and Jimmy was smiling broadly. Nancy, hatless and coatless, was making her way to the back of the house, looking fairly dazed.

Pollyanna dropped into a chair. Not more than two or three minutes passed before Jimmy made his appearance, but she felt as if she had spent half a life-time waiting for him.

Jimmy's face still wore that expansive grin.

"Well," he chuckled, "you need to remember that in a new country it's not safe to judge by appearances."

"What did he want?" gasped Pollyanna.

"Wanted the children to attend his Sunday school."

"What! It can't be—"

"Oh, yes, that's Sam Dobbs, our most exemplary citizen. He has organized a Sunday school that meets in the schoolhouse when the roads aren't too bad. I told him I was sure you'd help him."

"But why," Pollyanna demanded, "didn't he tell me?"

"A little shy, probably. Sam's an old bachelor, and his interviews with pretty girls are infrequent, I imagine. He'd rather sit on the porch and put it up to a man."

Pollyanna sat motionless. Then as she caught Jimmy's eye, the absurdity of her recent terrors flashed over her. She struggled for a moment against the impulse to laugh, since this was an implied acknowledgment that she had been ridiculous, but the impulse was stronger than her sense of dignity.

She began to laugh, and after assuring himself that she was not hysterical, Jimmy joined her. The children hearing the reassuring duet, rushed in and laughed with their parents, without knowing why. And Jiggs, snatching a dish towel from Nancy's hand, bounded into the room and ran around in circles, to demonstrate his ability to enter into the family mood, whatever it might be.

Pollyanna's laughter, while serving as a safety valve after her hours of strain, was not altogether enjoyable. She laughed till the tears ran down her cheeks. She laughed till her breath failed her and there were pains in her chest, and a heaviness like suffocation.

It was a hilarious ending to a harrowing afternoon, but her laughter failed to obliterate from Pollyanna's mind a really important lesson, that in her new home, even more than in her old, it was decidedly unsafe to judge by appearances.

CHAPTER IV

THE MOUSETRAP

AMONG the books which Pollyanna had brought with her was a bulky volume of quotations, and before she had been in her new home a month, she looked up a saying she vaguely recalled as credited to Emerson. The Sage of Concord, or some other observing person, had said that if a man could make a better mousetrap than his neighbor, though he built his house in the woods, the world would make a beaten path to his door.

It was not of mice nor of traps that Pollyanna was thinking, so much as of Dorothy Blythe. The girl was in a part of the world utterly new to her, living in an isolated ranch house, with no dwelling in sight. There were no neighbors near enough even, for the smoke of their morning fires to be visible, thin columns against the sky, misty but reassuring, since they told of human proximity and potential helpfulness. Yet, though Dorothy had withdrawn to so lonely a spot, there bade fair soon to be a beaten path to her door, trampled hard by the feet of young men.

45

Jimmy had really started it when he brought Clifford Wright home with him one Saturday. Wright was one of his lieutenants, a nice, shy, rather plain young fellow, who one immediately thought would be good to his mother and a prime favorite with old ladies. Realizing that as Wright was situated, a holiday would be a bore, rather than a welcome interlude, Jimmy invited him home for the weekend, warning him that he might have to sleep on the floor, rolled up in a blanket. "But there'll be plenty to eat, and somebody to talk to, to say nothing of the kids. They're great youngsters, Wright."

"I'm sure they are, Mr. Pendleton, and it's mighty good of you to ask me," Wright said, flushing with pleasure. "If you haven't any other place to put me, I'll sleep in the car." Although he spoke so earnestly, he had no idea how much he would enjoy himself. Jimmy had not thought to mention Dorothy, and so his guest was unprepared for meeting a demure young person who looked surprisingly like a child, but whose resourcefulness in the way of entertaining a diffident youth proved her maturity. By four o'clock Sunday afternoon, Pollyanna saw just what was going to happen. Indeed she had been afraid of it ever since breakfast, when she had noticed that the two young people were calling each other "Clifford" and "Dorothy."

It was the Pendletons' third weekend in their new home when Clifford Wright was added to the circle, and a few days later Pollyanna found another young man on her porch and deep in conversation with her governess. Dorothy introduced him prettily. He was, it appeared, a forest ranger, and his name was Hale. And before Pollyanna had quite recovered from her surprise, the cowboy appeared. He was not at all like the other two. For one thing, he was decidedly better looking than either, and in the second place, he was not in the least shy. His name was Leroy Fitzgerald, but he told Dorothy that everyone called him Jerry, and Dorothy showed her approval by making immediate use of that snappy nickname.

The young man on the train, Pollyanna realized, had been merely an incident, but that brief acquaintance had revealed Dorothy's idiosyncracy. She was a born coquette. Wherever she went, there would be young men trailing after her, and she would encourage each of them in turn, without ever seeming to think that this might mean suffering for somebody.

"If she'd only fall in love with your nice Mr. Wright, and let the others alone," Pollyanna confided to Jimmy, "I'd be easier in my mind."

Jimmy yawned. The cowboy had stayed late,

and as they were sleeping on the porch, they had been obliged to sit up till he took his departure. "Oh, well, it's nothing to worry about," Jimmy said philosophically. "Where there's a reasonably good-looking girl, there are bound to be young fellows hanging around. I don't know what they see in her, though," he added.

"You wouldn't," Pollyanna mocked. She was perfectly aware that she herself comprised Jimmy's ideal of feminine beauty and charm. Jimmy could never see what there was in other women to arouse anyone to enthusiasm. She went on to explain the reason for her uneasiness.

"I know Dorothy doesn't mean it, but she really is a terrible flirt. She acts as if she found each man who comes near her perfectly absorbing. That is the way she acted with the young man on the train. I was really afraid she would decide to go on to San Francisco and get married. Of course it's a weakness—flirting, I mean—but on the whole I think we're awfully lucky, don't you?"

Jimmy did not commit himself and Pollyanna repeated her question. Again there was silence and after a moment she understood why. She laughed softly and turning on her pillow, followed her husband's good example.

Other men appeared at intervals, but, for the

most part, they were errant comets, flashing into the field of vision, and flashing out again, apparently discouraged by the amount of competition they encountered. But the three original admirers were in the category of the fixed stars. No one of them showed the least inclination to withdraw in favor of his rivals.

Clifford Wright had the advantage of being on intimate terms with the head of the house. Jimmy asked him over frequently for weekends and he was so considerate and appreciative, such a jolly playmate for the children, and such a prime favorite with Nancy, that his welcome was always assured. The ranger avoided Sundays, after learning that this was the time he was most likely to encounter Wright, but he turned up once or twice a week, sometimes arriving by mid-afternoon, and always staying for dinner. Fitzgerald was the most uncertain in his movements of the three, but Pollyanna had an uneasy suspicion that when he did make his appearance, Dorothy was especially glad to see him.

"She couldn't be foolish enough to fall in love with Jerry, could she?" Pollyanna asked Jimmy, and added, without waiting for his answer, "That would be such a calamity."

Jimmy chuckled. "When you and I fell in love, my dear, of course it was all according to Hoyle.

But there are people who don't reason things out the way we did. They simply follow their hearts."

"You may laugh as much as you like," Pollyanna replied with dignity, "but I maintain that our falling in love was the most sensible thing we ever did."

"Sure it was, and that's the reason we did it."

"But this Jerry," persisted Pollyanna, ignoring her husband's attempt to divert her thought from a growing anxiety, "would make a very unsatisfactory husband, I'm afraid. In the first place, he doesn't earn enough to support a family."

Jimmy agreed with her. "No, he doesn't. It would be hard enough for a girl who had never known anything but hardship, but for Dorothy it would be impossible."

"And then he impresses me as such an uncertain person. Just as you think you understand him, he does something that astonishes you. He's good-looking, of course."

"Yes, you'll have to hand him that," Jimmy acknowledged. "He's good-looking and he knows it, too. He's as vain a pup as I ever ran across. It sticks out all over him."

"Then you admit that it would be an awful thing for Dorothy to fall in love with him."

"I can't discover anything especially hopeful in a good half of the love affairs I know about, but I don't see how that gives me a right to interfere."

Pollyanna did not share his scruples. She improved an early opportunity to drop a hint to Dorothy herself, and found her surprisingly frank.

"He's such an amusing creature, Mrs. Pendleton, and so different from anybody I ever saw before. He just fascinates me. After he's been here I always feel as if I'd been to the circus."

Pollyanna was sympathetic. "Yes, I understand. But isn't it a little dangerous to see so much of a fascinating young man, if he isn't just the sort of person—I mean if he hasn't the qualities—"

As Pollyanna groped for a tactful phrase, Dorothy came to her assistance. "Oh, Mrs. Pendleton, you don't suppose I'd think of marrying him? Really, that's the funniest thing I ever heard of!" She gave herself up to laughter, but Pollyanna's face remained grave.

"You ought to think of him, too. He might not see the ridiculous side of your acquaintance. It's not quite fair, is it, to lead him on?"

Dorothy leaned over and patted her hand. "Dear Mrs. Pendleton, you think of everybody, don't you? But don't worry about Jerry. He's just a born show-off, and it's a treat to him to have a new audience. He loves to practise all his arts on a new girl, don't you see, and that's all it means."

"I hope so," Pollyanna said, but she was far from reassured. Of course there were men like that, as there were women to whom love was all play-acting, who never took any affair so seriously as to lose a night's sleep because of it. This handsome, swaggering young fellow might belong to that class, but Pollyanna doubted it.

If her remonstrance resulted in putting Dorothy on her guard, there was no change that Pollyanna could see. Young Fitzgerald was a frequent caller, and one morning he appeared bright and early leading an extra horse, and invited Dorothy to accompany him. He had been sent to look for some strayed cattle, and had bethought himself of this ingenious way of combining business and pleasure.

"You'd better take along some grub for yourself, Kid," he told Dorothy. "We mayn't be back till sundown. I'm used to skipping a meal or two every now and then, but I guess it would be tough on you."

"I don't even know that I can go," Dorothy informed him petulantly. "Mrs. Pendleton doesn't pay me to spend the day riding over the country." But nevertheless she sought Pollyanna out, and stated the case, making an unsuccessful effort to appear dispassionate.

"If he'd asked me beforehand, I'd have told him no. But now he's brought a horse for me, and I suppose he'll feel insulted if I don't go. Perhaps I really ought to teach him a lesson. He's too cocksure, isn't he?"

Pollyanna looked into the girl's eager face and her own was troubled.

"I'd be glad for you to have a day's fun, Dorothy. I know you don't have many chances here. If you're sure it's wise—" But Dorothy had not waited beyond the first sentence. Already she was hurrying off to tell Jerry. It was past dinner time when she returned, stiff from her ride, complaining dolefully of pains in her back, and yet radiant. On principle Pollyanna objected to being a wet-blanket, but that night she did a good deal of thinking.

There was no doubt that Dorothy had earned a day off. In addition to her other duties, she was acting as chauffeur, and doing it well, but since she had not contracted to drive a car, Pollyanna felt it incumbent on herself to master the art. In a sense it was not difficult. If she had plenty of time to think, she could tell what to do under given circumstances, as correctly as Henry Ford himself. Unluckily, on the road one did not always have time to think, and if hurried, she was as likely as not to step hard on the accelerator, when she meant to use the brake.

Since learning to drive was no longer optional,

Pollyanna devoted an hour a day to practise, driving around the house, up the road, changing gears, reversing, turning, her face so set and grim that on one of the rare occasions when Jimmy acted as her instructor, he assured her she looked as if she had made up her mind to run over the first pedestrian she encountered. But it would be some time, Pollyanna felt sure, before she could drive with a smile.

Until she could trust herself at the wheel, she depended on Dorothy for their not infrequent trips to the nearest settlement boasting a post-office. The Rural Free Delivery favored them only twice a week, and as it was out of the question to wait from Tuesday to Friday for mail, Pollyanna fell into the way of driving to Deer Creek rather frequently in the afternoon, when the children had finished their lessons for the day, and before it was time for Jimmy to come home. Deer Creek considered itself a town. To Pollyanna it appeared a street about a block and a half long, lined on both sides with dwellings and primitive shops. There was a smithy, a filling station, a moving picture theatre where once a month or so a film was shown, and the post-office. In addition there were two general stores, one on either side of the street. The variety of their stock might have seemed amusing in an age when even shops specialized, but to Pollyanna, accustomed to the infinite variety of the city department store, there was nothing absurd in the juxtaposition of granulated sugar and talcum powder. She did wish, however, that the proprietors were a little more far-sighted, for one or the other was always getting out of something she wanted, and if she crossed the street to the rival establishment, she was always received with an air of hostility.

They reached the post-office one afternoon rather later than usual, and for that reason Dorothy and the children did not leave the car. Pollyanna got her mail, and hurried into the Emporium next door to make some trifling purchases. She secured what she wanted rather promptly, and was on her way to join the others when she found the passage blocked by a girl who stood before the door, looking out through the glass.

She was apparently a girl about eighteen. She was rather handsome, or at least, thought Pollyanna, she would have been handsome, had not her face been disfigured by a scowl. Yet she looked not so much like a victim of habitual bad temper as one who at the moment was experiencing emotions of the liveliest hate.

Rather startled, Pollyanna looked across the girl's shoulder and through the glass, not quite sure what she expected to see, but fully prepared to discover

something malignant or revolting. It gave her a
shock to perceive that the girl's attention was riveted
on her own car. The two little girls were on the
back seat, and practically invisible from where she
stood. Junior on the front seat nearest them, was
holding Jiggs, who at the moment was indicating an
unreasonable desire for a close acquaintance with a
lean wolfish dog accompanying an Indian woman, the
latter with a papoose hanging between her shoulders. And beyond Junior sat Dorothy, watching
the Indian woman with a curiosity as keen as
Junior's own. Her pretty profile was toward them,
and her air of unconcern made it clear that if she
were the object of the hostile scrutiny, she did not
know it.

Pollyanna looked up the street and down. Then
she looked again at the girl with arms akimbo,
barring her way. There was no possibility of a
mistake. She was looking straight at Pollyanna's
car, her brows drawn into a scowl, her lower lip
protruding. It seemed to Pollyanna she was breathing hard.

"Excuse me, but may I pass, please?"

The girl spun around. As she faced Pollyanna,
her color blazed. She had looked positively dangerous a minute before, but now, in her flaming con-
fusion, she was almost pathetic. More to set her at

ease than because she needed assistance, Pollyanna said smilingly, "I wonder if you'd mind opening the door for me? My hands are so full."

For a moment she almost thought the girl would refuse. But on second thought she turned the knob, and slammed the door open. Then disregarding Pollyanna's thanks, she turned and scurried back into the store. Pollyanna, glancing back, was astonished to see that the business of the Emporium had come to a standstill, while clerks and customers watched the byplay at the door. She had a confused feeling that her mystery was no mystery to them.

As she opened the door of the car, Jerry's face came before her. It was unlikely that Dorothy was the first girl to recognize the fascinations of that handsome young daredevil. It was more than likely that Jerry was the explanation of that look of helpless fury on the girl's face and the amused watchfulness of the others. Pollyanna sighed.

"I guess you're thinking 'bout King Herod, aren't you, Mother?" Judy demanded.

Pollyanna turned a bewildered gaze on her offspring. "What did you say, dear?"

" 'Bout King Herod. When I think how he killed all those dear little babies, that never did him a bit of harm, I feel as if—as if I could *shake* him, don't you, Mother?"

CHAPTER V

THE FAMILY GROWS

WHEN the Western dwelling had been decided on, Pollyanna mentally legislated against pets in her new home. Transporting them presented serious difficulties, and leaving them behind meant heartache. Jiggs, it was true, had succeeded in accompanying the family and, so far, without serious consequences, but Pollyanna was still assured of the wisdom of her first decision, and she made up her mind that the little bulldog should not be required to share with any other animal the perquisites attached to the post of household pet.

Then late one afternoon when Jimmy drove to the door and alighted from the car, he lifted out a limp, long-legged creature that slumped against his shoulder like a fainting woman. Pollyanna who was sewing on the porch, sprang to her feet and hurried to meet him. The children, too, came running from various points of the compass, and Jiggs arriving, ears erect, set up an excited barking.

"Oh, Jimmy!" Pollyanna looked down into two big, blank eyes which apparently had faced too many

terrors longer to reflect fear. "It's a young fawn.
What ails it?"

"Pretty near starved to death, I should say,"
answered Jimmy. "There's a good deal of hunting
around here I'm told, in spite of the game laws, and
this little chap's mother may have been a victim.
We'll try him with some milk. I don't know
whether he'll take it from human hands or not."

But starvation proved more than a match for instinctive caution. When Pollyanna forced a spoonful of milk into the little creature's mouth, it swallowed feebly, and at once the deadly apathy of its
blank eyes was replaced by eagerness. It was not
long before it was struggling to get at the milk, and
Pollyanna went on with her feeding till Jimmy inter-
fered.

"Listen, dear, for a starvation sufferer, I believe
he's had enough. We can give him another meal at
bed time."

"The poor little thing is hungry still," Pollyanna
said pitifully. "How dreadful for such a baby to
be left to starve. Jimmy, how can people shoot anything as gentle and helpless as a deer?"

Jimmy chuckled. "Seems to me I've heard you
express a longing for lamb chops recently. And there
can't be any lamb chops without a slaughter of the
innocents."

"I know," Pollyanna admitted dolefully. "I wish I could be a vegetarian. It's really embarrassing to have to own you belong to the carnivores—disgusting word, isn't it? But after all, Jimmy, killing animals for food is different from killing them for fun. It's terrible to me that nice people will shoot a beautiful animal like a deer and call it sport."

"I never cared for hunting myself," Jimmy replied. "But the shooting around here isn't for sport, you may be sure. They hunt for food just as our ancestors did. Now I'm going to put this little chap in the barn, and then we can have supper."

The meal was not over before young Wright appeared, carrying a small basket. He greeted Pollyanna with effusion and Dorothy with reserve, but Pollyanna noticed that while he talked to her, he kept a watchful eye on her governess.

"Mrs. Pendleton, I've brought you a pet. You like animals, don't you?"

"Another pet!" Pollyanna cried. "I believe you and Mr. Pendleton have been putting your heads together. You think I haven't enough to do, so you are just trying to furnish me with employment. Now, honestly, isn't that it? It can't be a mere coincidence."

The young fellow laughed. "I don't know what the boss has done, Mrs. Pendleton, but I'm acting on my own hook." He took from the basket a young crow, still in the rough, pin-feathery stage, and set it on his wrist. With preternatural solemnity, the little creature accepted the support, and sat motionless, blinking slightly as if in protest against being disturbed in its slumbers.

"Why, he's only a baby, isn't he?" cried Pollyanna, to whom infancy, even in feathers made a strong appeal. "Where did you find him?"

Young Wright grinned engagingly. "Well, I saw the nest on my way home, and made up my mind the old bird wouldn't miss one. I thought the children might like him, Mrs. Pendleton. I had lots of fun with a pet crow when I was a boy."

"Oh, I'm sure the children will like him," Pollyanna agreed, "Mr. Pendleton brought me home a half-starved fawn to-night. Now if I can get hold of a young coyote, and possibly a baby porcupine, my collection will be complete."

"You'd get in wrong with your neighbors if you made pets of either of those two," Wright told her. "The porcupine's a bad actor. Haven't you noticed how many of the evergreens around are dead at the top? That's because Mr. Porcupine has a fondness for the tender young growth. He helps himself and the tree dies. The rangers shoot every porcupine they see."

At the sight of the young crow, the children had lost interest in their supper. They gathered in a fascinated circle around the caller, and asked innumerable questions regarding the new addition to the family. "Will he peck us?" Judy inquired rather timidly.

"Bless you, no. This chap's only a baby, but even when he grows up he'll be friendly. They say that sometimes crows can be taught to talk."

"Ho! Birds can't talk," scoffed Junior. "You're kidding."

"How about parrots?" asked his father.

"Oh, I forgot parrots," Junior looked rather abashed, when his pretensions to wisdom were so promptly exposed, and was glad to have Judy divert attention from his slip, by asking eagerly, "What are we going to name our crow, Mother?"

"Dear me!" Pollyanna wrinkled her forehead in a pretense of agonized reflection. "What can we call him? The responsibility of naming three children almost turned my hair gray, and I believe a crow is even harder."

"And the fawn's got to have a name, too," Junior reminded her.

"Worse and worse. All this clever family will have to put on their thinking-caps and help me out. Anybody who doesn't suggest a name within five minutes by the clock, will have to pay a forfeit."

Thanks to this threat, suggestions were plentiful. When the young crow was tucked away in the basket for the night, his new mistress addressed him as Pluto, and when the fawn was fed for the second time, he was informed that instead of a nameless orphan, he had become Puck, and was an established member of the Pendleton family. Puck bore little resemblance to the limp, apathetic creature Jimmy had brought home in his car. He swallowed his milk greedily and butted his head against Pollyanna's arm, apparently under the impression that this would increase the supply.

"Lucky we decided to keep a cow," said Jimmy. "Looks as if this chap was going to develop a tremendous appetite."

"He needs to eat, poor dear, to make up for lost time," sighed Pollyanna. "See how his bones stand out." Then with a rapid change of tone from heart-felt sympathy to exasperation, "O Puck!" The exclamation was called out by the collision of Puck's head with a brimming spoonful of milk, the contents of which went flying in all directions.

"You wouldn't think it possible for one spoon to hold so much milk," lamented Pollyanna, ruefully surveying her bespattered dress. "You'd swear it was a cupful, at least."

"Next time you'd better wear a rubber apron,"

Jimmy suggested. "Try again, and I'll do my best to hold him steady."

In front of the house a small enclosure had been set off from the rest of the ranch by a picket fence. It was hard to associate the thought of Mrs. Schroeder with anything as frivolous as raising flowers, yet Pollyanna was tempted to believe that a vague notion of flower beds, secure from the onslaughts of chickens, must have been in her mind when the picket fence was erected. Pollyanna had disapproved of the fence on principle, but now she realized that its aesthetic lack was atoned for by its practical advantages. The small plot of grass surrounded by the picket fence, seemed providentially designed for Puck.

"He can't get out and wander away till he's old enough to take care of himself," Pollyanna explained to the children. "But if you see any strange dogs around, call Mother right away. The dogs out here may not be used to pets."

"Will Jiggs hurt Puck, Mother?" Judy inquired anxiously.

"Oh, I think not. But we'll keep an eye on him till they have a chance to get acquainted.

Pollyanna's feeling that Jiggs was not above suspicion was intensified by the dog's interest in the new acquisition. Instead of following the children to the porch, where the morning's lessons were in progress, and lying stretched at Junior's feet, while he struggled with problems in bank discount, Jiggs stood by the picket fence, gazing with grave scrutiny at the strange animal on the other side of the palings. Whether Puck was too young to realize that a dog was something to be afraid of, or whether, after his rescue from starvation by the Pendletons, he concluded that hereditary prejudices were unworthy of him, Pollyanna could not decide. It was certain that while he seemed as curious concerning Jiggs as Jiggs was concerning him, he showed no trace of fear.

"Don't you dare hurt Puck, Jiggs," Pollyanna warned the little bulldog. "I suppose it is hard to have your nose out of joint when you had every reason to think you were going to be our only pet, but at the same time, if you nip Puck's nose I shall punish you severely, yes, severely," she reiterated, as Jiggs turned his inscrutable eyes upon her, "and when I say it, I mean it."

When she saw him a little later standing up against the palings as if to get a better view of the fawn, she started toward him with the intention of administering discipline. Then abruptly she halted. Jiggs' tail was wagging. If it taxed one's credulity to believe that the dog was making friendly advances to the captive fawn, the evidence of that wagging tail was, from Pollyanna's standpoint, unanswerable. Whatever Jiggs's faults, he was not double-faced. A wagging tail did not conceal hostility. Pollyanna was sure of that. She drew back a step and breathlessly watched the drama unfolding before her eyes.

Had Puck's mother been beside him, she would undoubtedly have warned him against accepting overtures of friendship on the part of any canine. But sometimes youthful intuition has the better of cynical experience. And apparently the friendly treatment of these strange bipeds had given Puck a sense of confidence in all created things.

Step by step the fawn approached the fence against which the dog stood on his hind legs, panting excitedly and wagging his tail. A soft nose wriggling in an interrogative fashion was thrust into the triangle formed by two pickets and two great wistful eyes looked out at Jiggs.

Jiggs responded gallantly. His pink tongue flicked the quivering nose, which was instantly withdrawn. But kisses are much the same among the four-footed and after his recoil, Puck seemingly accused himself of unworthy suspicion. Again he approached the fence. Again his velvety nose was thrust through the opening and received a friendly salutation. This time he did not bound away. The two little creatures stood eye to eye, as if seeking some way to bridge that gulf between the hereditary friends of men and a line that has little cause to love them. And then and there was the budding of a queer friendship, destined to have an end as tragic as its beginning was picturesque.

Pollyanna, knowing nothing of the future, was extravagantly pleased. "If a dog and a deer will make friends," she asked herself, "why shouldn't the lion lie down with the lamb? Little Jiggs, if there were more of your sort, we could have the Golden Age without waiting."

CHAPTER VI

A BRIGHT IDEA

THE short-comings of her new home, the lack of
the conveniences to which she was accustomed, and
what was almost as bad, its aesthetic deficiencies,
were constantly in Pollyanna's mind for the first
few months of her Western sojourn. And this
undercurrent of feeling accounted for her difficulty
in understanding the errand which brought a delegation to her door one day in the late spring. She was
out in front of the house, watering some trans-
planted ferns, when a dilapidated, mud-splashed car
came up the drive. It carried five passengers, all
women, though in years they ranged from a tooth-
less old crone, who was lowered to the ground with
considerable difficulty, down to a girl of sixteen or
seventeen.

They approached the house in a compact group,
their manner a curious blending of daring and
timidity, and Pollyanna knew intuitively that an
aggressive gesture would have put them all to flight
like startled deer. Needless to say, she made no such

gesture, but went smiling to meet her callers, her cordial aspect concealing a very real wonder.

The middle-aged woman, walking a little ahead of the others, had evidently constituted herself spokesman of the party, and while at some distance she called, "Would you mind us lookin' round?"

"Certainly not," replied Pollyanna, though at heart she was somewhat perturbed. Could it be that someone was thinking of buying the ranch, and that before she was fairly settled, she would be obliged to start on a hunt for new quarters?

Rather to her surprise, the women went on past her toward the house. They paused at the door, and the spokesman faced about, while the girl giggled nervously.

"Do you mind us goin' upstairs? We want to see the bedrooms. I've heard tell that they're—" she searched for a word and brought it out with a smack—"that they're wonderful."

It took Pollyanna a moment to realize that her modest little home was regarded by these new neighbors of hers as a veritable show-place. This reputation must be due to Mrs. Schroeder, she reflected, since no one else had seen the upstairs rooms, and Pollyanna was convinced that Mrs. Schroeder, even while she fired the curiosity of her listeners, had scornfully repudiated any personal interest in anything fine. Brief as the pause was during which she adjusted herself to the novel idea, she atoned for it by a distinct increase in the cordiality of her manner.

"Why, of course, you may see them. Shall we go right up? Some of us sleep on the porch you know, but there are two bedrooms on the second floor."

As she started to lead the way across the living-room, the youngest member of the party caught sight of the bookcases, one on either side of the big fireplace. The girl stopped short. "Mother!" she cried, her voice fairly cracking in her excitement. "Look! Just look!"

They crowded around with murmurs of amazement. "Well, well, that sure is a sight," mumbled the old woman. "I ain't never seed so many books, settin' side by side, like a lot of guineas roostin' on a bough, not sence I was born."

"You don't mean to tell me," the spokesman of the party exploded, looking hard at Pollyanna, "that you've read all those books, an' you not much more'n a girl."

"No, I haven't read nearly all of these," Pollyanna acknowledged. "My friends thought I'd have considerable time for reading, and they advised me to bring along lots of new books. Sometimes I wish I hadn't followed their advice. I rather miss my old

book friends, the ones I've read almost to pieces."
She gave them time to look their fill, but when the
old woman oracularly expressed her opinion that
"books and buttonholes was hard on the eyes," she
accepted the remark as a signal to go upstairs.

There were twin metal beds in each of the rooms
on the second floor, and Pollyanna had tried to dis-
guise their natural ugliness by fitting each with a
valance of dotted muslin to match the window curtains. There were rag rugs on the floor, a bureau
and a wash stand in each room, and some com-
fortable-looking willow chairs, with bright cretonne
covers and cushions. The furnishings had been so
inexpensive and the effect was so far from luxurious, that Pollyanna was quite prepared to have her
visitors disappointed when they contrasted this modest reality with their bright anticipations. So far
from being disappointed, however, they stood rapt.

The oldest woman was first to find her voice.
"Well, it's a sight," she cackled, showing her tooth-
less gums in a wide smile. "I'll be eighty come
August, and I ain't never seed beds rigged out with
white starched petticoats, not sence I was born."

"Which one's your room?" one of the women
asked, speaking quickly, as if she feared Pollyanna
might consider the reference to petticoats a criticism.

"Oh, I sleep on the porch. My good Nancy and

little Ruth have this room, and Miss Blythe and Judy the other."

She saw a quick exchange of glances at the mention of Dorothy's name. She was conscious of electricity in the air. "Miss Blythe," the voice repeated. "She's the short-haired girl, ain't she?"

"Yes. I'm sorry she's not here this afternoon. When we don't drive to the village, she generally takes the children for a walk."

"Is she kind of a hired girl, or what?"

"She teaches the children. We're so far from the school, you see, that there would be many days they couldn't attend. So we have a teacher for them at home." Pollyanna felt somewhat disturbed by the turn the conversation had taken, and by the certainty that all had been discussing Dorothy. She moved over to the girl who stood by one of the beds, looking down at it with a curiously wistful expression.

"The valance dresses it up, doesn't it? And they are really very little work and not at all expensive."

"Lots of extra washin', though," said one of the women who had not spoken before, and Pollyanna was sorry to see the girl's look of interest die out, like a flickering flame quenched by a timely dash of cold water.

Their curiosity as to the bedrooms satisfied, they found plenty downstairs to discuss. The dining-room, when once they understood its purpose, made a deep impression on them all. "She keeps a whole room jest for eatin' in," wheezed the old woman. "I'll be eighty come August, and I ain't never heard o' sech doin's, not sence I was born."

"It must be a lot o' extra work, carryin' things from the kitchen way in here, three times a day, and then cartin' 'em back again," said the woman who had spoken upstairs of the extra washing. She was a thin, wiry creature, with a dogged mouth, and tired eyes. Pollyanna guessed that in her busy days, every extra step had to be considered.

"Yes, it does make more work," she admitted. "But don't you think people eating in the kitchen are rather in the way?" And again she was aware of an exchange of glances, a shared amusement, like that called out by some impractical suggestion made by a child.

Pollyanna would have omitted the kitchen from the tour of inspection, if the decision had been left to her, but the delegation advanced upon it, like soldiers charging without orders. As usual the girl brought up the rear, something in her expression suggesting that she was not quite satisfied as to the propriety of the visit. Nancy, busy ironing, turned on the intruders a blank face, which the most optimistic could not have pronounced cordial.

"Nancy, these are some neighbors of ours," Pollyanna said. "And I shall have to ask their names before I introduce them."

"You ain't a-goin' to hev as hard a time as you think," chuckled the old woman. "Three of us is Murrays. I'm Mrs. Hannah Murray, an' this here—" she pointed to the woman who objected to extra work—"this here is my daughter-in-law what married my son Joseph. The girl's my granddaughter, Mattie. All three Murrays. You kin kill three birds with that one stone."

She laughed over her joke till she coughed, and had to be patted on the back, and after the commotion was quieted, the woman who had asked permission to see the house, announced that she was Mrs. Dunn, and that the shadowy fifth, who so far had not said a word, was Mrs. Geist. As neither statement was contradicted, Pollyanna proceeded to introduce Nancy.

Nancy nodded as each name was spoken and uttered a gruff, "Please to meet yer." Unfortunately, as her manner showed only too plainly, she was anything but pleased. Nancy considered the call an unwarranted intrusion, and particularly resented, Pollyanna was sure, the influx into her kitchen. She stood grimly silent while the visitors examined the new stove, and the kitchen cabinet, and called one another's attention to the rocking-chair. Some time later when Pollyanna took a meal at the Murray home, and noticed that all the members of the family sat on packing-boxes, she understood why the rocking-chair in Nancy's kitchen occasioned so much comment.

Pollyanna guessed that the investigations in the kitchen would have been more thorough had not Nancy's demeanor acted as a check. She knew what was passing in her mind, as well as she did after the visitors' departure, when Nancy declared that it was all she could do to keep from ordering them out of the room. "Gawpin' 'n' pryin' 'n' stickin' their noses where they had no business to be," cried Nancy. "I wonder if these folks out here call such goin's-on manners." But it was not only Nancy who was critical. Far and wide through the valley had spread the rumor that the Pendleton's hired girl did not eat with the family. Five pairs of curious eyes looked Nancy over, wondering that so poor-spirited a creature should appear so much like an ordinary self-respecting woman.

Pollyanna welcomed the distraction when there was a loud squawking just outside the door. "Land sakes, ef that don't sound for all the world like a crow," one of the callers cried.

"And that's what it is," replied Pollyanna. "Our

pet crow." She opened the door, and without waiting for a further invitation, a lusty young crow fluttered into the room, and gave the group the benefit of a searching scrutiny. When Pollyanna held her wrist invitingly down before him, he accepted it as a satisfactory perch, and sat there composedly, while she lifted him to the level of her shoulder. Then catching sight of the bread Nancy had baked and set to cool, he flapped his wings and cawed loudly.

Pollyanna attempted to explain her pet to the silent guests. "A young man who comes here occasionally found the nest, and brought me one of the young birds. He was a lot of work at first, but now he eats everything. We call him Pluto."

Still silence on the part of the visitors, and with the uneasiness most of her sex feel over a conversational lapse, Pollyanna rattled on, "We're getting quite a menagerie already. A few weeks ago, Mr. Pendleton brought home a young fawn. The poor little thing was almost starved, but it's in fine shape now. And the queerest friendship has sprung up between the fawn and our dog. It's real fun to watch them."

"Be you goin' to raise that there pest?" demanded old Mrs. Murray, pointing a denunciatory finger at Pluto, and voicing, it was only too plain, the thought in the minds of them all. "If there's one livin' thing that's jest a plain nuisance, it's a crow."

It was Pluto himself who saved Pollyanna the necessity of replying. He put his head on one side and looked inquiringly at his critic. Then he cawed again, and his manner was so defiant, that Mrs. Geist for the first and last time during the afternoon was startled into an exclamation.

"He knows all right you've been callin' him names," Mrs. Dunn declared. "There's more'n just plain bird under those black feathers. I wouldn't have that there crow in my house for a million dollars."

It occurred to Pollyanna that a cup of tea all around might relieve the tension. Nancy's teakettle was ready to boil as soon as it was pulled to the front of the stove, and Nancy had made gingersnaps that morning, and there was a crock of them, crisp, spicy and delicious. Pollyanna marshaled her visitors into the dining-room and served them promptly. She had a feeling that she was chattering absurdly, but whatever sterling qualities these ranch women possessed, they were lacking in small talk. They drank their tea, munched their gingersnaps and listened—whether indulgently or critically was not apparent—to Pollyanna's efforts to be entertaining.

But before they left, something destined to have

far-reaching consequences happened.   Pollyanna noticed that Mattie Murray was again standing before
one of the bookcases, gazing wistfully at the rows
of volumes.   Pollyanna went over to her, and Mattie looked up with a shy little smile that warmed
Pollyanna's heart.   That smile conveyed the welcome information that whatever was true of the
older women, Mattie was no longer afraid of her.

"If I ever get rich," said Mattie, in a breathless
rush of confidence, "that's what I'll have, a whole
lot of books."

"You won't have to be very rich for that,"
laughed Pollyanna.   "The first birthday present I
gave Mr. Pendleton after we were married was a
set of Dickens, and we were anything but rich then.
I wanted to bring that set of Dickens along, but he
wouldn't let me.   He's very particular about those
books."

Mattie's eyes had widened as she listened.   "Do
you mean you've got more books somewhere else?"

Instead of answering the question, Pollyanna
asked another.   "Wouldn't you like to borrow one
of these?"

"Borrow one?"   Mattie looked as blank as if her
hostess had been speaking in an unfamiliar tongue,
and Pollyanna found herself under the necessity of
explaining.   "You can take one home to read if you

like. Then when you have finished, bring it back, and I'll let you have another."

Mattie only stared, apparently unable to believe that the offer was meant seriously, and Pollyanna left her to wrestle with her incredulity, while she herself scanned the rows of books. "I'll pick out a good one," she promised gaily, and after a moment, selected a volume she had packed with a vague idea that Judy might enjoy it. "There," she smiled. "I'm sure you'll have a good time with that."

Mattie clutched the book greedily, even while she began to stammer disclaimers. "I wasn't hinting, Mrs. Pendleton. I didn't mean—"

"I know that, my dear. But as long as you like books, I'm glad to share mine with you."

Absorbed in her conversation with Mattie, Pollyanna had not noticed that her other guests had joined them. They stood in a row just back of her, listening intently, and as she turned, old Mrs Murray spoke.

"We used to hev a book back home when I was a girl. It was about some kind of pilgrims, 'n' angels 'n' Heaven, 'n' I don't know what all."

"I have a copy of that very book, Mrs. Murray. Wouldn't you like to take it home and read it over again?"

Mrs. Murray's evident incredulity vanished at the

sight of the illustrations in Pollyanna's well-thumbed
copy of Pilgrim's Progress. "Yes, it's them," she
cried excitedly. "There's them very same angels,
lookin' just as nat'rel as life. I never expected to see
them angels again, not this side o' Jordan."

Mrs. Dunn found her voice. "I've got a girl
who's just crazy about readin'. Could she take that
book Mattie's got, when Mattie's finished with it?"

"Yes, but she doesn't need to wait for that. I
have some others she'll enjoy just as well."

It was decidedly the most successful part of the
afternoon, Pollyanna decided, for with the exception
of the silent Mrs. Geist, all of them became fairly
voluble. And even Mrs. Geist, when asked if she
would not like a book for her invalid son, smiled
faintly and held out her hand for the volume which
Pollyanna assured her would be certain to interest
a boy.

"Not that Luke's a boy eggsactly," said Mrs.
Dunn, after waiting vainly for Luke's mother to
make the correction. "He's twenty-four, but I guess
he'd find most anything int'restin', shut up in the
house year in and year out."

Even before they left, Pollyanna's bright idea was
germinating, and by dinner-time it was in full flower.
She waited to announce her plan till they were all
at the table, having learned the wisdom of choosing

for such revelations a time when escape was difficult.

"Listen, everybody. I'm going to start a circulating library. Spots on the table cloth will be subject to a fine of one cent for children and five for adults. And we'll use the money for buying books. And then we'll all ask our friends to send us the books they are through with."

"I'll present you with the text books I used in college," offered Dorothy generously. "I've finished with them, I *hope*."

"They'd be useful to somebody, I don't doubt, but they don't fit in with this plan. I want the most interesting books that have ever been written. I know lots of people that will help. Aunt Ruth and Lorraine and Anne and—"

"You'll have to appoint a censor, won't you?" interrupted Jimmy. "It won't do to corrupt the morals of this valley."

Pollyanna's hesitation was momentary. "I'll tell them to send only nice books, of course. There really are plenty of them, though they're not talked about as much as the others. It's like the happy marriages. The people who quarrel and fight and sue for divorce get into the newspapers, and the happy couples are never mentioned. James Carew's books will be splendid, all but Growing Pains."

"You mustn't expect James to donate all his books

to your circulating library," warned Jimmy. "At that rate, authorship would be anything but profitable. What's the idea, anyway? Are you planning to add a little to the family income?" He spoke without the suspicion of a smile, though Pollyanna was sure he could not be as dense as he seemed.

"You know better than that, Jimmy Pendleton. It was really dreadful how excited those women were at the sight of our few books. You'd have thought it rivaled the Congressional Library. The oldest one, almost eighty, she is, said they'd had a book in her home when she was a girl, and it proved to be Pilgrim's Progress. I don't believe she's ever owned one since. Think of it!"

Nancy prided herself on knowing her place, as she phrased it, but this day had tried her beyond endurance. Unexpectedly she appeared in the doorway, and spoke her mind. "Folks as crazy 'bout books as all that had ought to buy 'em."

"Oh, Nancy, the people in this valley are poor. They haven't any money for extras."

Jimmy backed Pollyanna up. "Very few of the ranches are irrigated, and if they have a dry summer, as they did last year, it's hard to get through the winter."

"They got along somehow before Miss Pollyanna come," sputtered Nancy. "I don't know why she

should wear herself to death fixin' up liberries for
'em."

It was useless to protest. Nancy's affection constantly showed itself in the fear that someone was
going to impose on Pollyanna's kindness of heart.
She went back into the kitchen muttering to herself.
But Nancy was the only one to throw cold water.
Jimmy promised a money donation, in addition to
the fines he was sure to have to pay, and Dorothy
offered to write some of her college friends, and
ask them to send on such books as they did not
care to keep, and were suited to Pollyanna's circulating library. Junior nobly volunteered to lend his
Peter books and Judy, not to be outdone, offered her
Alice in Wonderland to the library, provided her
mother would stipulate that any little girl who read
it must wash her hands. Even Ruth was so carried
away by the spirit of the thing that she took a spoonful of her chocolate pudding, and deliberately ladled
it on the table cloth. "There!" she cried trium-
phantly. "Now I've got to pay a cent, an' you can
buy books with it, Muvver."

CHAPTER VII

LUKE

MRS. DUNN's reference to Mrs. Geist's invalid son, shut in the same small room, year in and year out, haunted Pollyanna. Those unforgetable months in her childhood, when she had been unable to walk, had given her a passionate sympathy for everyone helpless and suffering. It followed naturally that one morning when her work seemed less pressing than usual, she made up a package of magazines, and with Ruth as her sole companion, drove to the Geist ranch. It was her longest drive when the responsibility was entirely hers, and she felt it so keenly that when she reached her destination the perspiration stood in beads on her forehead, as if she had been toiling under a mid-summer sun.

Mrs. Geist came to the door as the car halted before the ranch house. If she was pleased to see her callers, she concealed her emotions admirably, for she only stared dumbly.

Pollyanna climbed from the car and lifted Ruth

to the ground. Then possessing herself of the package of magazines, she went smilingly toward the
silent woman in the doorway. "You see I'm return-
ing your call bright and early," she called.

Mrs. Geist's lips moved, but no sound escaped
them. It was rather as if she would have liked to
reply but had forgotten how.

"I brought these over for your son," explained
Pollyanna, indicating her burden. "Of course he
can't read all the time, but some of these magazines
are full of pictures, and I think he'll enjoy them."

Mrs. Geist turned and disappeared in the house.
It was apparent afterward that she had expected
her visitors to follow her, for when she looked back
and found that they were standing where she had
left them, she promptly retraced her steps and again
came into view, this time wearing a ludicrous
expression of surprise. Accepting this unspoken
invitation, Pollyanna took Ruth by the hand and
followed their hostess.

They made their way through the kitchen with
some difficulty, for the table was standing in the
middle of the room, with the breakfast dishes still
upon it. The ironing-board, one end resting on the
table, the other supported by several boxes piled one
upon another, occupied most of the remaining space.
A door at the further end of the kitchen opened

into a small, dark hall, and this, in turn, into Luke
Geist's room.

Pollyanna stood hesitating at the foot of the bed,
as Luke stared up at her. His hair had evidently
not been cut for months, for it fell almost to his
shoulders, and his face was covered with what appeared to be a three weeks' growth of beard. From
under the unkempt hair, a fierce young face glared
at her, the dark, resentful eyes challenging her presence.

Pollyanna, waiting expectantly for Mrs. Geist to
introduce her, discovered that the mother had again
disappeared, and with that realization, proceeded to
introduce herself. "I'm a new neighbor of yours,
Mrs. Pendleton, and this is my little daughter, Ruth.
I thought you might be interested in some of these
magazines. We all enjoyed them."

Luke pointed to a sagging chair. "Guess you
can sit on that without falling through," he said
gruffly. "The kid can sit on the foot of the bed or
stand up. It's all the same to me."

Pollyanna was pleased to find that Luke had not
inherited his mother's capacity for silence. People
might be disagreeable, or resentful, or denunciatory,
but if they put their feelings into words, there was
something to take hold of. The silent sort, locking
turbulent emotions back of sealed lips, was baffling.

She sat down cautiously, as the chair looked as if it might collapse at any moment, and Ruth, choosing the second of the alternatives Luke had offered, crept close to her mother, gazing with fascinated eyes at the strange-looking figure on the bed. Pollyanna was not sure just how to open the conversation, but as she settled herself in the rickety chair, and glanced through the window, a topic instantly suggested itself. "Oh!" she cried with an enthusiasm in which there was no make-believe, "What a lovely view!"

Luke's lips twisted into an unpleasant smile. "Like it, do you?"

"It's beautiful. I thought the view from our front porch was perfect, but this is even finer."

"Glad you think so," Luke sneered. "I've been looking at this view just four years, three months, and twenty-three days, and if you want to know, I'm getting pretty sick of it."

An involuntary shiver went over Pollyanna, as she pictured him lying there, keeping relentless count of the hours as they dragged by. But she said as casually as possible, "It isn't always the same view, though."

"What d'ye mean?"

"Well, it's one view in summer, and something else in spring, or fall, or winter. It's one thing on a sunny day like this, and another when it rains. It's one view now, and at sunset it'll be quite different."

"Oh," acknowledged Luke grudgingly, "if *that's* what you mean, it is."

"I used to go to see a woman," continued Pollyanna, "who had lain on her back in the same room for twenty years. There was a window in the room but the house was so close to the next one, that all she could see was the brick wall."

Luke grunted. "Twenty years, eh? Well, I hope I can find some way to cut my throat before I've been here twenty years."

"She didn't feel that way," said Pollyanna. "She seemed a very happy woman."

At the sound of the young man's discordant laughter, Ruth pressed closer to her mother's knee, taking a firm hold of her arm. Pollyanna herself had been startled.

"Happy, was she?" snarled Luke, his laughter stopping as suddenly as it had begun. "That's a good joke."

"It's very wonderful, I know. But it's true."

"Guess she was one o' the lazy sort," scoffed Luke. "Liked lying abed, and being taken care of like a baby."

"No, that wasn't it. But she was very sympathetic. From all over the neighborhood, people came to tell her their troubles."

"Their troubles, hey? What about hers?"

"That was the strange part. She never spoke of her own troubles. She thought of them, I suppose—"

"You bet she thought of 'em," Luke interrupted. "Anybody in our fix has lots of time for thinking, you see. All the long days when other folks are busy and can't be bothered, and all the long nights when other folks are asleep. And all the time she was thinking, she wished she knew a lot of good, strong swear-words, so she could tell God what she thought of Him."

If he had counted on shocking Pollyanna, nothing in her manner gave him reason to think he had been successful. She answered simply, "Perhaps so, but I'm inclined to believe she spent her time thinking of pleasant things."

"Pleasant things! Pleasant things! That's all you know about it. What's so durned pleasant about lying on your back and staring at the ceiling?"

"Well, there are always some pleasant things, aren't there?" Pollyanna asked diplomatically. "Perhaps she liked to think of the people she had helped. I remember going there once when a mother and daughter were in the room, and both of them were crying. They had quarreled, and hadn't spoken for years. But both were friends of this sick woman, and at last she had succeeded in getting them to make up."

"That's your idea of a good time, is it? Women sitting 'round sniveling. Wouldn't excite me none."

"Well, it made her happy to know they were friends again, thanks to her. And then, too, people were always doing friendly things for her, and it was wonderful how much fun she got out of every little kindness."

"She sure was born for that kind of life," commented Luke acridly. "Well, it don't suit me."

A figure appearing in the doorway, quickly recoiled. Luke raised his voice, and checked what was apparently an impulse to flight.

"Hey there, Min Walker! What you afraid of? Nobody here's going to bite you."

As if encouraged by this assurance, the vanishing figure again materialized. It stood in the doorway, red and defiant, and Pollyanna instantly recognized the girl she had seen in the store, gazing at Dorothy with such unmistakable hostility. Perceiving that introductions were considered superfluous in the Geist household, she said pleasantly, "I remember you very well. You opened the door for me one day in the store, when my hands were full of parcels."

"Oh, Min's always doing kind things," mocked

Luke. "She even comes 'round to see me sometimes, and there ain't many girls who'd bother. But you see you're not needed here today, Min. Somebody got ahead o' you."

"What did you call me back for then?" the girl flashed. "I don't care about butting in where I'm not wanted."

"I'm sure," protested Pollyanna hastily, "that a new friend can't be nearly as welcome as an old one. Please come in. I must be going very soon anyway."

"I've got to see Mrs. Geist about something," retorted the girl, still aggressive. "Maybe I'll come back, and maybe I won't." She flounced off tempestuously, and Luke favored Pollyanna with a malicious grin.

"She's pretty sore, Min is. She's crazy about that Fitzgerald, and he liked her all right till you folks come along. That girl at your house has got him going, and now Min's ready to stick a knife in somebody. Girls are sure fools."

Not wishing to subscribe to the ungallant sentiment, and yet not quite sure she would be justified in denying it, Pollyanna remained silent. But Luke did not need the encouragement of a reply. It was evident that he found the presence of a stranger exhilarating, a welcome break in the intolerable monotony of his life, and he talked on, disregarding her silence.

"Take the way they fall for Jerry. He's got looks, all right, and he sure can ride, but other ways he ain't so much. Maybe you'd expect Min to lose her head over him, but that girl at your house—well, it's durned funny she should be as crazy about him as the rest."

"Dorothy Blythe is a very friendly girl," said Pollyanna, choosing her words carefully. "She seems to like almost everyone. But as far as I know, there is no one she likes especially."

"Better not tell Fitzgerald that. He's not used to being an 'also ran.' He thinks he's bound to be the whole show, if he wastes his time on a girl. It don't matter a durn how many strings he's got to his bow, he expects to be ace-high with every girl in the bunch."

Pollyanna decided to change the topic of conversation. She felt rather guilty to be discussing Dorothy's love affairs with a stranger, and she wondered, too, if this bedridden boy in a lonely ranch house might possibly know better than she did just how far the affair had progressed. She asked casually, "Did your mother tell you about my pet-exhibit the other day?"

"Who? Ma? She don't tell much. If you want

to find out anything from Ma, you need a fish-hook. What kind of exhibit did you say it was?"

Pollyanna explained, and went on to tell in some detail the story of Pluto and the fawn. She was not sure whether she was boring her listener or entertaining him, but his languid voice, when he asked a question, made her fear that he had found the recital dull.

"What's the idea, feeding a crow? Sooner all them pests are dead, the better."

"Well, anyway he's lots of fun. You know a crow is as smart as any bird that flies. Some of them learn to talk ."

"Oh, come off!"

Pollyanna suppressed a start, and then, perceiving that Luke intended no impertinence, persisted good-humoredly, "Indeed they do, and they are full of amusing tricks. Haven't you any pets at all?"

"What, crows?"

"I was thinking of a dog."

"Well, we did have a dog once, but he worried the cattle and we thought he did as much harm as good."

"I was only thinking that a dog would be so much company for you."

"Company for me! What would be the good of a dog to me, shut up the way I am?"

Pollyanna recalled Jimmy's comment on the fact that in this part of the world, little sentiment was wasted on dogs. "My dog is company for me," she said, "and you are alone so much."

"Oh, you meant to have him come into the house? Ma'd never stand for that. Besides, I don't know what good it would do. You can't talk to a dog."

"I can," laughed Pollyanna.

"Oh, well, you can talk to a stick of wood, if you feel like it, but it can't answer you, and no more can a dog."

"Mine does," Pollyanna insisted. "You wait and see. I'll bring him over some day."

It was time to go, she decided. Gradually she was coming to the conclusion that Minnie Walker would not return till she herself had taken her departure. She was gratified to perceive that as she stood up, Luke's face clouded over.

"Well, I guess I've seen the last of you. 'Tain't likely you'll come back."

"Why do you think that?" smiled Pollyanna, more encouraged by this bit of gruffness than by anything he had previously said.

"Not much fun here. Now you've seen the worst looking scare-crow you ever set eyes on, outside a field of grain, I guess you'll be glad to forget what he looks like." To Pollyanna's horror he gave his attention to Ruth. "Say, kid, how do you like my looks?"

Pollyanna checked her instinctive impulse to clap her hand over Ruth's mouth, and drag her from the room before she could answer. Bitter experience had taught her Ruth's fatal frankness. But since Luke had asked the question, there was nothing to do but to allow Ruth to reply, and pray that her answer might be obscure if not diplomatic.

"I fink," said Ruth, in her high-pitched, childish voice, "that you're a funny man."

"Funny? Why am I funny?"

" 'Cause you look like my dolly Jocko."

Pollyanna's blood froze. Jocko, of course, was not a doll at all, but a velvety monkey, with a bristling black beard, an abominably life-like creation. She stood appalled, while Ruth laughed consummately, squeezing her eyes tight shut in the intensity of her enjoyment.

"Didn't know I was so durned funny as all that," Luke looked rather dashed, and Pollyanna, thankful to have him spared the full import of Ruth's reply, said good-by, and hurried her daughter away before he could ask that outspoken child another question, the answer to which was bound to be embarrassing.

She made her way through the kitchen, looking vainly for Mrs. Geist. Minnie Walker stood scowling in the doorway, and though she moved aside to let Pollyanna pass, it did not seem a courtesy so much as an effort to expedite the process of getting rid of her.

"I don't wonder Jerry prefers Dorothy," Pollyanna said to herself as she drove away, and the involuntary thought roused her to the realization that the acquaintance of Jerry and Dorothy presented a serious problem. The handsome young fellow had evidently been a rural lady-killer, capturing feminine hearts with as little compunction as if they had been so many butterflies. The embittered girl, who had transferred her resentment from Dorothy to Dorothy's employer, was, it was plain, desperately unhappy, a victim to a coquette's craving for excitement.

Or was this all? Pollyanna recalled that on her first meeting with Dorothy, the girl had declared she would rather see a cowboy than a king. Could it be that in spite of her modern sophistication, Dorothy was as susceptible to the lure of romance as the most guileless maid of the derided Victorian era? And if so, what could be done to save her from herself?

Pollyanna caught herself up sternly. After all, she was passing judgment without full knowledge of the facts. She was hardly better acquainted with

Jerry than with the woodlands birds which, flashing into her range of vision and out again, left a
vague impression of exuberant spirits and pic-
turesqueness. Pollyanna believed ardently in the
power of love. If there was something in Jerry
that appealed to the real woman in Dorothy, long
submerged by the coquette, then possibly their best
chance for happiness was with each other.

"I must know that boy better," Pollyanna told
herself. "In a sense I'm responsible for Dorothy.
She never would have met him if it hadn't been for
me. Perhaps I can't accomplish anything, but at
least I can find out what I want to do, and that's
more than I know at present."

CHAPER VIII

A DINNER PARTY

I⊤ was not Pollyanna's way to postpone putting a resolution into effect, and when she drove up to her home, and heard an assertive masculine voice holding forth on her front porch, she felt the time had come for action. She greeted the children, quieted Jiggs who, like most dogs, welcomed the members of the family after the briefest absence, as if they had been gone for weeks and given up for lost. Making her way to the front of the house, she at once was aware that her appearance was an interruption. Dorothy's poise was perfect as a rule, but today she flushed hotly. And Jerry, who evidently had checked himself in the middle of a sentence, gave Pollyanna the impression, even as he greeted her gaily, that he wished her a thousand miles away.

"Good afternoon, Mr. Fitzgerald." Pollyanna disregarded the high color of her governess and the young man's air of resentful embarrassment. "I wonder if you can arrange to take dinner with us next Saturday at half-past six."

The instantaneous change in Jerry suggested the

passing of the sun from a state of total eclipse.
"Sure thing!" he cried. "When I get a bid to dinner, you bet I can arrange it any old time."

"That's good. Then I'll expect you Saturday."

"Look here, Mrs. Pendleton," Jerry exclaimed,
as Pollyanna, her errand finished, turned to enter
the house. "Don't go to putting any handle to my
name. When anybody calls me Mister, I think he
wants to borrow money from me. I'm plain Jerry
to my friends."

Dorothy was looking startled. Without being
blessed with any especial intuitive faculty, she had
reached the conclusion that Pollyanna was uneasy
over this fast-growing intimacy. And now apparently, she had changed completely, and had made
up her mind to lend the affair her official sanction.
It was characteristic of Dorothy that at once she
felt it imperative to proceed with caution. It was
one thing to walk and ride with this romantic young
man, who looked like a movie star, and quite another to have their acquaintance tacitly recognized
by an invitation to dinner from the mistress of the
house. While Pollyanna lingered, the girl contrived
to smile mechanically, but when Jerry and she were
alone again, her lips straightened without her realizing it.

"Cute little trick," commented Jerry, looking after

Pollyanna as she went lightly into the house. "But what put her up to ask me to grub? I'll bet you had a hand in it, girlie." And again it was characteristic of Dorothy that she did not deny the accusation, undeserved as it was.

That was Thursday, and it was not till Saturday that Dorothy's vague apprehensions took a more definite form. She came into the dining-room about the middle of the afternoon, and found Pollyanna setting the table. Dorothy looked it over critically.

"The children are going to have their dinner in the kitchen about an hour ahead of us," Pollyanna explained. "This will be a real party."

"Who's coming besides Jerry?" questioned Dorothy, an edge to her voice.

"Clifford Wright will be here, and Mr. Hale, too. You're bound to be a belle, Dorothy, only one girl, and three young men."

"It'll be quite a responsibility, won't it?" smiled Dorothy, but her feeling of uneasiness was not dissipated. The average coquette prefers to see her admirers one at a time, and Dorothy was no exception to the rule. But that did not altogether explain the feeling of apprehension with which she awaited the dinner hour.

They did not sit down till past seven, after all, for Jerry was half an hour late. When he walked into the house, they understood why. He had made a fancy dress toilet in honor of the occasion, and wore such resplendent chaps that one felt he must have escaped from a Wild West show. Jerry fully appreciated the fact that he was a magnificent spectacle. He stood grinning for a moment, before he swept off his wide-brimmed hat.

"Thought I'd give the girls a treat! Some rig, eh?"

Jerry swaggered into the dining-room, his handsome head held high. He was well aware that he eclipsed the other young men, who were only moderately good-looking, and wore business suits, commonplace in contrast with his own romantic costume. His sense of satisfaction was increased by the discovery that he was seated between Pollyanna and Dorothy. It gave convincing evidence that Mrs. Pendleton, after being a little stiff and stand-offish, had fallen for him at last.

As Jerry took his place, he scanned the table critically. There were flowers in a centre vase, and at each place a low glass containing cut fruit. This with the napkins, tumblers and silver was all, and Jerry thought it a bare and uninviting board. He planted his arms on the table, and turned to Pollyanna. "Now, look here," he said, "Is this the way you feed hungry folks back East?"

"That's the way we start out," smiled Pollyanna, picking up her spoon.

Jerry studied the contents of the cup. "Kind of mixed, ain't it? A guy'd hardly know whether it was something to eat, or—not!" he finished with a suggestive smile.

The remark received less than its due. Nobody laughed, but Dorothy's face flushed to the roots of her hair. With elaborate unconcern, Jimmy commented on the lateness of the season, and Clifford Wright seconded him with all haste. Jerry's eyes went the rounds of the table, and came to rest on Dorothy who was devoting herself to her fruit cup.

"What's the matter, girl?" Jerry was totally unabashed by the failure of his joke. "Put my foot in it, did I? It's either that, or nobody in this bunch has a sense of humor."

"Undoubtedly the fault is ours," Dorothy replied so icily that Pollyanna, who had been feeling very sorry for her, at once felt sorry for Jerry. She was not prepared to have him turn to her with his engaging smile.

"Look here, Mrs. Pendleton, guess you'd better steer my talk a little. Looks as if I was getting in wrong all 'round."

"Shall I raise my eyebrows at you, the way I do with Junior?"

"That's all right for a kid, but it takes something
stronger for a cowboy. Couldn't you squeeze my
hand under the table cloth? The boss is too far off
to know what we're doing."

Dorothy had lost interest in her meal. She addressed a remark to young Hale, and gave him her
absorbed attention as he answered. Jerry looked
up knowingly. Pollyanna saw he could hardly wait
for the other young man to finish what he was
saying.

"Don't get sore, girl!" he begged, when Hale gave
him a chance to speak, "just because I'm going to
let Mrs. Pendleton squeeze my hand. I've got another hand, you know, and you're welcome to that."

Dorothy's impressive silence was rather embarrassing to them all. It was a relief when Nancy
began serving the soup. As Jerry noticed she was
bringing one plate at a time, he leaned confidentially
toward Pollyanna.

"Say, want me to lend the old girl a hand?" he
asked, as Nancy disappeared into the kitchen. "It'll
take her all night at this rate. I reckon she's afraid
of breaking something, if she takes a reg'lar load."

Pollyanna liked him the better for his offer,
though she declined it hastily. "Thank you, but
it would hurt Nancy's feelings if you offered to
help her." She saw Dorothy's face coloring again,

and was sure that Jerry, too, had noticed it. She was realizing her wish to get better acquainted with Jerry, but her success made her uncomfortable. Though she had acted from the kindest motives toward both young people, she was depressed by an unwonted and unwarranted sense of guilt.

She might have spared her sympathy as far as Jerry was concerned, for by the time the soup was served he was again dominating the conversation. He told a story of an encounter with a wolf, and told it well, but he blew on his soup to cool it, and swallowed it noisily. And when at the close of his really thrilling narrative, he told a banal story of a whiskered individual and a plate of soup, Dorothy's embarrassment communicated itself to everyone at the table.

When the roast was brought in, Jerry was the only one with heart to make conversation. "Say, this is one of those to-be-continued-in-our-next kind of dinners. I was just wishing if you was going to give us soup, you'd give us a little more, and here's a man-sized piece of beef. Now is there anything more coming that I've got to save room for, or can I eat all I want?"

"You'd better do justice to this course," Pollyanna encouraged him. "There won't be anything more except the salad and dessert."

"Salad and dessert! O boy!" Jerry whistled piercingly. "Some dinner, I'll tell the world." Then as Nancy brought him the dish of potatoes, and stood waiting for him to help himself, he addressed her directly. "What do you expect me to do? Take all I want, or just one?"

Nancy's disapproval expressed itself in stony silence, and Pollyanna came to the rescue. "Nancy always prepares plenty, so it will be your own fault if you leave the table hungry." She tried not to notice how many potatoes Jerry was piling on his plate, but she could not turn away her fascinated eyes. Was he demonstrating his rather uncouth sense of humor, she asked herself, or could he actually dispose of that mound of potatoes?

Jerry relinquished the serving spoon after everyone's nerves were taut with the long suspense, and Nancy went back to the kitchen to replenish her supply, before serving the other men. But without waiting for them, Jerry attacked his meal, telling breezy reminiscences as he ate, and unfortunately doing most of his talking when his mouth was full.

Pollyanna was sure by now that after-dinner coffee would excite Jerry's risibilities and her expectations were realized. He regarded his small cup with a perplexity that seemed quite sincere.

"What's all this, Mrs. Pendleton, a sample?"

"They are rather small, I know," Pollyanna acknowledged, aware that Dorothy had made a movement expressive of irritation. "But if they're filled often enough, they are as good as the large ones."

"Why, that's no more than a swallow." Jerry raised his cup to his lips and emptied it at a gulp. He pushed it toward her with a boyish chuckle. "If it's all as good as the sample, I'll have some coffee." He repeated the witticism half a dozen times before they adjourned to the living-room, but Dorothy, asked if she would have more coffee, refused almost witheringly.

Once away from the table, Jerry appeared to better advantage, Pollyanna thought. He still did most of the talking, but he did it well. It was true that he had no scruples over interrupting the others, and if they had the bad taste to continue talking when he showed he had something to say, he raised his voice and drowned them out without a qualm. But in spite of his numerous *gaucheries,* Pollyanna saw he was making a rather good impression on her husband. Jimmy and he fell to discussing the probable effect of the new dam on the future of the country, and Jerry showed himself not only fluent but capable of real thinking. Hitherto, Jimmy had recognized only the young fellow's good looks and his naive vanity, but something in his manner betrayed a new respect for Jerry's ability. Pollyanna wished it were as easy to know what Dorothy was thinking as it was to read Jimmy's mind.

Dorothy was quieter than Pollyanna had ever known her to be. Even her flirtatious instincts seemed dormant. The presence of three young men, all of whom were her avowed admirers, failed to move her to a single coquettish gesture.

Wright and Hale left about eleven o'clock, Jerry lingered longer, hoping, Pollyanna felt sure, for a few minutes alone with Dorothy, a privilege the girl seemed disinclined to grant. Jimmy, with his customary obtuseness in such matters, made no move to leave the room, and placidly continued the conversation he had found so interesting. And at length with obvious reluctance, Jerry rose to take his leave.

"Well, folks, guess it's time I was getting a move on. Ladybird here looks like she was ready to drop off to sleep."

Dorothy smiled thinly. It was a question, Pollyanna reflected, whether she would sleep at all that night.

Jerry shook hands all round. "Some swell feed," he complimented Pollyanna. "It ain't often a cowboy breaks into high sassiety. Didn't see me eating with my knife, did you?"

"I certainly didn't," said Pollyanna heartily, thankful that this particular enormity had been omitted from the list. And then as Dorothy uttered a comprehensive good-night, and ran up the stairs, Pollyanna felt a pang of sympathy for the disappointed boy.

Dorothy's retirement had been strategic. As Pollyanna attended to those last imperative duties no housekeeper ever omits, and no one else understands, she heard the girl's feet again on the stairs. Dorothy came flying to the kitchen, and slammed the door shut. Meeting her flashing eyes, Pollyanna felt a sense of relief. She much preferred to talk the thing out, and this, she saw, was exactly what was going to happen.

"Mrs. Pendleton," Dorothy began in a strangled voice, "I wouldn't have believed you could be so unkind. It was cruel of you."

"Just what do you mean, Dorothy?" In spite of her astonishment, Pollyanna spoke with a calmness which seemed to infuriate the younger woman.

"Oh, you know what I mean, asking Jerry here to make him ridiculous. Setting a trap for him! That smug Clifford Wright! I suppose he and Hale are laughing yet."

"You mean, then, that Jerry can't stand comparison with the others without seeming ridiculous."

"I don't mean anything of the sort. He's twice
the man Clifford is. If they'd had the same advantages, no one would look at Clifford twice when
Jerry was around. He's a rough diamond, but
he's a diamond all right, and Clifford is nothing
but a piece of quartz. If Jerry had had a different
sort of home—"

"Are you trying to tell me that Jerry can't be
invited to an informal, friendly meal without being
put at a cruel disadvantage?"

Dorothy hesitated, then faced Pollyanna, her head
held high.

"Yes, I mean that," she said, "exactly that. And
what's more you knew just how it would be. You
went ahead and had the dinner served in courses,
and the coffee with the dessert, and you did it on
purpose to show him up. All the time you seemed
so friendly. I wouldn't have believed it of you."

Pollyanna had listened patiently, though her
cheeks were burning. "I don't think it should be
necessary for me to defend myself against such an
accusation," she said quietly. "Probably by morning you'll be ashamed of what you have said. But
your injustice to me isn't especially important. The
thing that impresses me is that you yourself realize
that Jerry doesn't fit into the life to which you are
accustomed."

"I don't see how that has anything to do with what we're talking about."

"I think it has," Pollyanna persisted. "Jerry is a handsome young fellow with a decided charm. When you see him in his rightful setting, there's a glamor about him. But marriage means three meals a day, Dorothy, and a girl brought up as you have been, ought to know something about a man's table manners before she decides on her husband."

Dorothy laughed shrilly, almost hysterically. "Husband! I never heard of anything so absurd. As if I'd think of marrying Jerry."

"You accused me of cruelty a minute ago, Dorothy. If you feel that way, and still are letting this acquaintance run on, you're the cruel one. If Jerry hasn't a chance, you're doing wrong."

This time Dorothy's laughter was spontaneous. "Mrs. Pendleton, I've told you before there's no need to worry about Jerry. He's a born flirt himself. I'm a mere novice at the game beside him."

"I hope you're right, but I doubt it. I'm anxious on his account and yours, too. He has a fascination for you that might easily carry you off your feet. I want you to know what you are doing, that's all. If you want to marry a man you'd be ashamed of at your own table—"

"According to you," the girl interrupted savagely,

"the most important qualification in a husband is knowing what fork to use for his oysters at a formal dinner."

"That's rather exaggerated, isn't it?" Pollyanna's calmness was a pretense, for her pulses were hammering. "I do think that as many marriages go to smash over a difference in tastes as over a difference in convictions. But as far as Jerry's manners are concerned, you are the one who has been criticizing them—rather severely, it seems to me."

Dorothy hesitated, then turned and flounced from the room, again shutting the door hard. And Pollyanna turned to Jiggs, who, his head on one side, sat listening to the dialogue with that air of comprehension characteristic of the dog who knows himself one of the family. As if she was confident both of his sympathy and understanding, Pollyanna addressed him.

"If she takes it so to heart, Jiggs, it is high time something happened. My party didn't turn out just as I expected, but I believe it's fair to call it a success."

And Jiggs wagged his tail, as if quite agreeing with her.

CHAPTER IX

GETTING MATTIE STARTED

It was characteristic of Dorothy that after the outburst in which she accused Pollyanna of setting a trap for Jerry, she came down to breakfast next morning, cheerful and smiling, apparently without a cloud on her spirits. Undoubtedly many women would have resented the translating of their kindly motives into cruelty, but Pollyanna's friendliness suffered no decrease. At the same time, she resolved to keep a wary eye on her governess. As she had suggested to Jiggs, the fact that Dorothy was so upset by Jerry's poor showing at a friendly dinner proved how deeply she was interested in the young man. The demonstration Pollyanna had staged had been eminently successful from one point of view, but the effect on Dorothy herself was doubtful.

She found plenty to occupy her thoughts and fill her mind as she practiced her watchful waiting. Pollyanna's Eastern friends had responded nobly to her appeal for her library. Almost every day a package of books arrived, some of them worn and shabby, showing unmistakably that they had con-

tributed to the entertainment of many readers, and
others were practically new. The classics were well
represented, and the latest writers were not over-
looked. Pollyanna examined the latter contributions
with especial care before she let any of them out
of her hands. It was astonishing how many books,
pronounced daring by certain critics, impressed her
as incredibly cheap and vulgar, and others, praised
for style and characterization, presented so base a
picture of life that Pollyanna wondered how anyone
believing in the truth of such a picture would care
to go on living. She had a number of little private
bon-fires, due to these unfortunate selections, and felt
quite relieved when nothing was left of the pages
that had revolted her but clean ashes.

Jimmy had aided her project by ordering an extra
bookcase to be devoted to the circulating library,
and Pollyanna tacked an explanatory card to each
shelf, so that in case someone came for a book when
she was out, Nancy could act as librarian. Nancy
accepted this responsibility reluctantly. Nothing
could alter her conviction that Pollyanna's new neighbors were imposing on her when they borrowed her
books.

Pollyanna soon learned that Mattie Murray was
the most ardent book lover in the valley. She was
a girl of surprisingly intellectual tastes, considering

that her education had not progressed beyond the district school. She worked hard at home, and up till the time of meeting with Pollyanna, she had enjoyed very few of the pleasures that are girlhood's right. But the first book she carried home with her opened the door into an enchanted garden. She had a headache the day she returned Ramona, and she confessed, after Pollyanna had done some tactful questioning, that she had cried most of the night after finishing it. A Gentleman of France so intrigued her that she hated to part with it, and read it through for the second time before she could bring herself to return it. Pollyanna soon realized that though she was only eighteen, her literary taste was more mature than that of most of the adults of the valley, and she took real pleasure in selecting for Mattie's reading, books that would supply the element so sadly lacking in her prosaic life.

On one of her visits Mattie took from the pocket of her coat a piece of wrapping paper on which was penciled a long list of words. "Mrs. Pendleton," she began, swallowing nervously, "have you got a-a- dictionary?"

"Why, yes, Mattie. Did some word bother you?"

"It wasn't a word," Mattie replied dolefully. She looked at her new friend with a blending of shyness and confidence. "It was a whole lot of words. Just look!" She held up the paper with a despairing gesture. "I didn't 'spose I was such a fool. It looks as if I didn't know nothing to speak of."

Pollyanna examined the list, and her face showed her pleasure. "Do you mean you wrote down all the words you didn't understand, Mattie?"

"Yes, and just look how many there are. But there isn't any dictionary at our house, so writing 'em down didn't do any good. I guess you didn't know what a dunce you was lending books to."

"Mattie, you couldn't have done anything that would please me more. Any one who will do what you have done is bound to become an educated woman some day. There's my dictionary over there on the stand, but when you're ready to go home, I'll have a little present for you."

Mattie hung over the dictionary for a long time. Now and then Pollyanna came into the room, and smiled at the girl's air of absorption. "Getting on all right?" she inquired on the third visit.

Mattie turned glowing eyes upon her. "Oh, Mrs. Pendleton, wouldn't it be wonderful to know all that is in this book? Just think of being sure what everything means. Oh, dear!"

Pollyanna laughed. "You remind me of the old lady who said the dictionary was such an interesting book, even if the story was somewhat disconnected. Come out into the yard when you have finished, I want you to see how Puck has grown."

It was some time before Mattie appeared, and even then, the spectacle of Puck, the fawn, and Jiggs, engaged in a game of tag, made little impression on her mind, still filled with the elusive meanings of various words. But when Pluto alighted on Judy's shoulder, and with incredible quickness dropped something down the little girl's neck, Mattie joined in the shout that went up.

Poor Judy shrieked again and again. "Oh, Mother, it's something that bites and scratches. O-oo-oo! And it's awful cold. O-oo-oo! Get it out quick!"

Pollyanna rushed to her daughter's rescue, impatiently brushing Pluto aside, as he fluttered around her, planning, it was evident, to alight on her shoulder. Hastily unbuttoning Judy's frock, Pollyanna pulled it off over the child's head. And as she did so, there fell on the ground not the toothed and slimy monster of Judy's description, but the little pewter teapot that belonged to one of Ruth's tea-sets.

Ruth's eyes widened as she recognized her treasure. She rushed to recover it, grasping it tightly in both hands, as if defying Pluto to recapture it.

"Muvver, he stoled it, that bad old bird!" She scowled furiously at Pluto. "My dollies had supper on the porch and he stoled my teapot away."

"Yes, he's a great thief. And he likes to play tricks on us, too. Poor Judy! What did you think had dropped down your neck, dear?"

"I thought maybe it was a horned toad, like the one in the natural history book." Judy, who had been on the verge of panic, giggled nervously as she slipped back into her frock. And Jiggs, sensing a crisis in the family life, left his friend, Puck, and came wagging back to human companionship.

Mattie Murray looked long at the group, the laughing faces of the children and their mother, Jiggs pressing close to Judy, who showed her appreciation of his sympathy by slipping a slender arm around his neck, the fawn nibbling grass in the background, Pluto perched on a diminutive plum tree. It seemed to her like a picture from a beautiful fairy book. Her expressive face clouded over. Unexpectedly the tears started to her eyes.

Pollyanna saw the changed look, the starting tears, without seeming to see them. She called to her son, "Junior, don't you want to take the girls over behind the big rock, and pick some of those yellow flowers for Mother? I want enough to fill two vases."

"Oh, all right." Junior stood very straight, flattered by the implication that his sisters were entrusted to his care.

"Jiggs can go too, can't he?"

"Of course. It would break your heart to be left behind, wouldn't it, Jiggs?"

Jiggs gave his tail a humorous waggle, suggesting that he would like to see anyone keep him from accompanying the children, and started off at a gallop. From his perch on the plum tree, Pluto saw the procession and with a loud caw, as if announcing his intention of joining the line of march, he flew in the direction the children were taking, alighting on a fruit tree, and waiting for them to overtake him.

Pollyanna watched the departure smilingly, and then turned to Mattie. "Well, my dear!" she put her arms about the girl's drooping shoulders. "What's wrong?"

There was a rather long silence which Pollyanna herself broke. "I didn't mean to seem inquisitive, Mattie," she said at length. "But I thought you were in trouble."

Mattie sighed tumultuously. "I don't know as I'm in trouble," she replied, speaking slowly, as if deliberating the question, "only—only some folks have such a lot of nice things, and then other folks don't have anything nice, not a single one, and it don't seem fair."

Pollyanna smiled at the unconcealed envy in the

girl's voice. Then she thought of her Eastern friends, who would pity her if they saw her in her present environment, and the term "relativity" took on a new significance.

"Everybody says it's just like having a party here all the time," Mattie continued, " and folks wonder how you can keep smiling always, as if something nice had just happened. But if I lived in a house like this, where everything was so perfectly grand, I'd feel like smiling, too."

"Well, Mattie, I've known people who had much more beautiful homes than mine who weren't a bit happy. After you've learned the secret, your cheerfulness won't be dependent on your surroundings."

Mattie knit her brows. "Do you mean," she said, "that I could be like you—happy and smiling and acting all the time as if everything was just grand?"

Pollyanna laughed at this description of herself. "Why shouldn't you do it as well as I?"

"You never were at my house," Mattie said, and seemed to feel she had answered the question sufficiently.

"No, that's true," Pollyanna admitted. "I'm going to come to see you some day, though. But don't imagine that I never saw anything like it before. My father was a home missionary in the West, and we were very poor, so poor that we never could buy the doll I longed for. Dear Father, when I think how it would hurt me if Judy and Ruth were begging for something I couldn't give them, I know just how he felt."

Rather to her surprise, Pollyanna felt the tears burning in her eyes. Mattie looked at her startled, and found it necessary to readjust certain ideas.

"But Father did something better than buying me a doll," continued Pollyanna, smiling again. "For he started me playing the Glad Game, and that meant finding something to be glad about, no matter how disappointing everything seemed. The children are always begging me to tell them about the time the crutches came in the missionary barrel."

"Crutches? What for?"

"Well, in those days, the churches in the East sent their missionaries out West boxes and barrels of partly worn clothing, and other more or less useful things. Sometimes the contents were hardly worth what the freight must have cost, though of course, it wasn't often as bad as that. This particular time that the children love to hear about, I had prayed very hard for a doll, and I couldn't see any reason for being glad when I found in the barrel a pair of little crutches, and nothing else especially suitable for a little girl."

Mattie's face wore a reflective frown. "But why did they send crutches? You weren't lame, were you?"

"No. I suppose the owner didn't need them and found them in the way, and so added them to the barrel on the chance that they would prove useful."

"And you said—but I guess I didn't understand you. You couldn't have said you were glad to get them."

"Not that exactly. But Father's Glad Game required me to find something to be glad about. Left to myself, I might have failed, but Father helped me to see that I could be glad that I didn't *need* the crutches."

"Oh, that!" said Mattie and sat thoughtful for a moment. "Do you feel that way about everything?" she demanded at length.

"That's my first impulse, thanks to Father. The game he taught me has changed my whole life. I've learned to look at things from a special angle, not for something to be sorry for, but for something to be glad about. And, Mattie, you'll find there's always something."

"You never were at my house," Mattie insisted doggedly. "There's nothing nice about it. And nobody has anything to say, and nobody ever laughs the way you do here. There's nothing nice at all—except your books."

"Well, then," smiled Pollyanna, "you can start with being glad for the books."

"Oh, yes. I'm glad of them," said Mattie quickly. She looked at her new friend with worshipful eyes. "And I'm glad of you. I didn't know there was anybody like you in the whole world. And to think of your coming here of all places!"

Pollyanna laughed out. "Well, if you ask me, I think you've made quite a start. Oh, I almost forgot. I promised you a present, didn't I?"

It took her only a moment to find what she wanted. She was back almost immediately with a small book, which she dropped into Mattie's lap.

"This isn't borrowed, you understand. It's yours to keep."

"Is it—why, it's a dictionary. Oh, Mrs. Pendleton!" Mattie's fingers were trembling as she fluttered the leaves. "Do you honestly mean this dictionary is mine for keeps?"

"That's what I mean. It's small, but it will be useful. And if ever you want to know more about a word than it tells, there's always my big dictionary to fall back on."

Mattie sat looking down at the little volume in her hand. She had a feeling not easy to describe, as if someone had given her a key that would unlock the door into a new and wonderful world.

Words! Everything that was to be known was locked away in words, but that did you no good, if the words themselves were mysteries. But now the key was in her hand. A dictionary of her own.

"Mrs. Pendleton!" Her face twisted grotesquely, as her contending emotions did battle, joy, wonder, gratitude, all striving for the upper hand. She heard herself whispering, "I don't know why you're so good to me." Secretly she wished for some catastrophe, some danger menacing this lovely lady, that she could rush to her rescue and die in her defense. Translated into words it was a grotesque fancy, but it embodied all the stifled poetry, the starved romance of the girl's nature. She wanted to fall on her knees and put her lips to the ruffle of Pollyanna's dress.

"Bless your heart, it's nothing," Pollyanna said, feeling the impact of the girl's surging emotion. "But I'm glad *you're* glad to have the dictionary. Seems to me you're making a good start on the Glad Game."

"O, yes'm, I'm glad," said Mattie, "as long as you're here, I guess there'll always be something to be glad about. And if you want me to, I'll try to play that game of yours. Only—you'll have to show me how."

CHAPTER X

"MANY HAPPY RETURNS"

POLLYANNA was wondering whether Jimmy would remember her birthday.

Of course she hoped he would. There is something distinctly flattering in the assumption of your friends that a certain day in the year is of paramount importance because you first looked on the world on that particular date. But Pollyanna told herself sternly that she must not take it to heart if he forgot about it—as had sometimes happened. Jimmy was a thoughtful and considerate husband three hundred and sixty-five days out of every year, and since that was the case, he could be forgiven an occasional lapse of memory where her birthday was concerned.

If Jimmy remembered that the ninth of the month was an important occasion, he would make her a present, of course, and Pollyanna wondered excitedly what it would be. Birthday presents always excited Pollyanna, even those purchased at the Five and Ten. There was something thrilling in having people racking their brains to find out what you really wanted, and then doing their best to gratify that desire. If Jimmy did remember her birthday, she hoped he had noticed that she needed a new manicure set.

On the evening of the eighth, Jimmy looked up from the book he was reading and addressed her. "By the way, Pollyanna," he began.

Pollyanna's heart gave a bound. When Jimmy said, "By the way—" that elaborately casual form of address—it always meant he had something special on his mind. "Yes, Jimmy," she answered eagerly.

"I wonder if you wouldn't like to drive over to the dam with me tomorrow morning, and look around a bit. We've been doing things since you were there last, and the trip would make a little change for you."

He *had* forgotten then. Of course it would never occur to him to suggest her leaving home on her birthday. It was true that the children might be as forgetful as their father, but if Junior happened to notice a calendar, he would be almost sure to recall that the ninth was his mother's birthday. Even Judy knew the date well enough, though she was less likely than Junior to consult the calendar. And if they discovered that it was her birthday, and that she had left them to go on a jaunt with their father, they would feel aggrieved and rightly.

It was sheer good luck that just at that moment Pollyanna discovered she was going to sneeze. A sneeze is a peculiarly engrossing process. One sneeze almost always means three and sometimes more, and the pauses between are not favorable to explanations. But even while one is devoting one's self to a fit of sneezing, one can do considerable reflecting. Pollyanna sneezed five times, and was thinking hard through it all.

Whether Jimmy had forgotten her birthday or not, he was planning for her pleasure. And, moreover, he had a pride in the work he was doing and looked forward to impressing her with its success. All good mothers find themselves tempted at times to put their children's claims before the claims of their husbands. Between the first sneeze and the fifth, Pollyanna had decided that if Jimmy wanted her to spend the day with him, that was his right.

Apparently Jimmy had forgotten his invitation. He was staring at her with an expression of consternation. "Good Lord!" he exclaimed. "Where did you pick up such a cold?"

"I don't think I have a cold."

"Darned good imitation, I should say. Better take something."

Pollyanna wiped her eyes and blew her nose. "I'll be glad to," she said.

"What do you mean?"

"I will be glad to go with you tomorrow."

"Oh, that. Well, we'll see how you are. You might be coming down with something, sneezing twenty times in a row."

"Don't exaggerate," Pollyanna reproved him. "There were only five."

The five sneezes proved to be all. Pollyanna felt sure they had nothing to do with a cold in the head, but were a providential interlude, giving her a chance to change her mind.

It was clear that the children, too, had forgotten her birthday. In the morning nobody wished her many happy returns of the day. They were all rather painfully eager to help her off. Even little Ruth warned her, "Better hurry, Muvver," when Pollyanna stopped for a word with Pluto, who always flew for her shoulder when he first saw her in the morning.

" 'Out of the mouths of babes,' " quoted Jimmy, who was no more patient than other husbands, when it was a question of starting somewhere.

"Coming, Jimmy. Good-by, darlings. Don't let the children out of your sight, will you, Dorothy. Good-by, Nancy. No, Jiggs, you can't come this time."

Jimmy pushed her into the Ford and shut the door while she was still uttering her last injunctions. And when once the ranch was left behind, Pollyanna found her spirits rising. She was ashamed of herself, but she had felt a little hurt over the fact that no member of the family had remembered her birthday. But the morning was so beautiful, the air so exhilarating, and Jimmy such a handsome and agreeable comrade, that before they were fifteen minutes from home, Pollyanna was congratulating herself that Jimmy had hit on this novel and delightful way of celebrating her birthday. The fact that he had planned it without remembering what day it was added to her enjoyment. It was a rather long drive to the scene of Jimmy's labors, but Pollyanna was in a mood to wish it twice as long.

When they reached the site of the proposed dam, she found everything of absorbing interest. A good deal had been accomplished since her last visit, and her exclamations of surprise and delight gave Jimmy as much pleasure, apparently, as if she had been a brother engineer. The men looked at her curiously as she walked at Jimmy's side, and the sight of her slender figure and glowing face brought to more than one the memory of some loved woman, perhaps the width of the world away.

Pollyanna missed one friend. "Where's Clifford?" she inquired.

"Oh, Cliff's not here this morning. Had some freight to look after."

They had brought their luncheon, with coffee in the thermos bottle, and Pollyanna was astonished to find herself ravenous. "You poor boy!" she exclaimed sympathetically. "I feel in my bones that we haven't been giving you half enough to eat."

"You'd have heard from me in that case," Jimmy assured her. "But there's no doubt that this air does put an edge to the appetite."

Luncheon over, Pollyanna stretched herself in the shade, while Jimmy went for a necessary interview with the camp cook. The next thing she knew he had her by the shoulder and was shaking her gently, while he laughed in her face.

"Wake up, Sleepyhead, wake up. Next time I'll bring an alarm clock."

"Oh!" Pollyanna sat up blinking. "I must have had forty winks."

"Forty! Forty thousand, more likely. It's time to go home."

"Jimmy, you don't mean you've let me waste all my—I mean all my lovely afternoon, sleeping."

Jimmy chuckled. "You talk as if it were all lost time. When I came back, you seemed to be enjoying yourself so hugely that I hadn't the heart to wake you. Besides I'm making a rather early start."

Pollyanna did not ask him why. She was less inquisitive as she was still absorbed with the grievance of having slept away so much of the only birthday she would have for a full year. But when they were again in the car, and facing homeward, her spirits underwent a characteristic rebound. If the freshness of the morning had been delightful, the golden shimmer of the afternoon seemed to her equally appealing. The fact that they were headed for home, and that the children were waiting for them made the afternoon drive even more enjoyable than that of the morning. Out of sheer lightness of heart Pollyanna hummed a little tuneless song, and glancing at Jimmy found him regarding her with a smile.

"A penny for your thoughts, sweetheart."

Pollyanna was nothing loth to tell them. She gave his hand a little pat before she explained, "I was just thinking that everything was so beautiful—and we have such good times—and, well, I just wondered why I was so lucky."

Pluto was the first of the household to greet them on their return. He came flying toward the car when the ranch house was as yet invisible. "There comes Pluto," cried Pollyanna.

"How do you know it's Pluto? All crows look alike to me," exclaimed Jimmy.

"I know it's Pluto because he's coming to meet us."

"You don't suppose he'd recognize us at this distance."

"It may be telepathy," said Pollyanna cheerfully, "but he always comes to meet me. If Dorothy is out with the car, he leaves her to drive in unattended, so it isn't the car he recognizes. See! He's coming down."

"Well, I'm blessed!" Jimmy exclaimed incredulously, but Pluto's downward swoop left no room for scepticism. He perched on the top of the car and cawed loudly, though whether he was complaining of something that had happened during her absence, or was merely saying that he was glad to see her back, Pollyanna had no way of knowing.

Considering that she had only been away a few hours, Pollyanna felt that she should be flattered by the exuberance of her welcome home. The children came rushing to meet her, and Pollyanna noticed the little girls had on fresh frocks and that Junior was resplendent in his Sunday trousers. Jiggs was frisking about, holding one of Pollyanna's galoshes in his mouth, and trying hard to bark without dropping it.

Pollyanna, walking into the house by the back-door, caught sight of the dining-room table and stopped with a gasp. There was a big frosted cake in the centre of the table, such a large cake, and so elaborately frosted, that there could be but one explanation for its presence, even if it had not been for the telltale circle of candles. Her birthday had not been forgotten. Jimmy's invitation was merely a ruse to get her out of the way while certain preparations were going on.

"Oh, Nancy!" she cried as enthusiastically as if she had been no older than Judy. "What a wonderful cake!"

"Guess it ain't none too good for you, Miss Pollyanna, wishin' you many happy returns."

"Muvver peeked," Ruth declared reproachfully.

"Oh, Mother!" exclaimed Judy, seizing Pollyanna's hand. "We've only got twelve candles for your cake. We thought it would cost too much to have a candle for every one of your years."

Pollyanna laughed, and was about to assure her daughter that twelve candles were quite sufficient when Junior interrupted gruffly, "Oh, say, come on! What are we stopping for?"

They went on into the living-room and saw against the wall a natty little cabinet which had not been there when she left. Clifford Wright, who had suddenly become master of ceremonies, walked up to it, turned a knob here, and another there in a knowing fashion, and all at once an invisible baritone was right in the room with them, singing "Mandalay." Pollyanna was rude enough to interrupt the music.

"Why, Jimmy—Jimmy Pendleton, you've always said—"

"I know I did. When we were a few minutes' ride from a big city, I couldn't see a radio at all. But it's different out here, and especially in winter. We can hear symphony concerts in New York and lectures in Boston, and keep in touch with what's going on in the world wherever it is. Think you're going to like it?"

"Jimmy!" Pollyanna spoke in a dazed voice. "I think it's the most wonderful idea that ever was. Of course you've been dreadfully extravagant and I shall have to scold you some day, but I'm too happy to do it now. When there's something extra fine, Jimmy, we can ask people in to listen. At least we've got our memories, but nobody around here ever heard a symphony concert. I'll just love to see Mattie's face. Oh!"

The change in her tone was so unmistakable that all her listeners cried in chorus, "What's the matter?"

"I was just thinking," said Pollyanna, dolefully, "that the person who needs the radio most can't come. Poor Luke Geist, you know."

"Yes, I know; too bad," Jimmy said, but perhaps

his mind was on something else, for to Pollyanna his sympathy seemed casual.

"Just think what it would mean to him, Jimmy, bed-ridden and lonely, with that queer, silent mother of his the only person within reach most of the time, and not even a dog to keep him company. If only he could share this with us."

"Yes, I know," said Jimmy again. "But I'm afraid that is impossible and please don't let your sympathy run away with you, dear. You look as if it wouldn't take much to make you cry, and I was trying to give you pleasure."

"If you see me crying, it will be because I'm bursting with happiness," Pollyanna assured her husband and went over to kiss him.

Good as the birthday supper was, they did not linger long at the table. Even the resplendent cake was cast in the shadow by the new radio set. In less than an hour they were back in the living-room, listening enchanted while Clifford twirled the dials, locating stations, cutting off pompous orators in the middle of sentences, tuning out a singer so ruthlessly that her single high note seemed a shriek rather than a song. It was quite exciting to hear from so many large cities in such quick succession, but Pollyanna resolved that when she was manipulating the dials, everyone should have a chance to be heard.

It was long past the children's bed time, and Pollyanna had twice yielded to their impassioned plea to
sit up "just a little longer," when an automobile horn
honked outside and a voice called, "Hello, the
house!"

"It's Hale, isn't it?" exclaimed Jimmy, starting
up. "Now I wonder—"

Junior had rushed to open the door and Hale
walked in smiling. "Good evening, everybody.
Mrs. Pendleton, I was looking up some express that
was over-due, and I found a package for you, so I
brought it along."

"Oh, how kind of you!" Pollyanna jumped to her
feet, looking at him eagerly, as if she expected him
to produce the package in question from his pocket.

The young man laughed "It's out in the car.
Guess I'll need some help in getting it inside."

Jimmy started toward the door, but Clifford was
ahead of him and as the two disappeared, Pollyanna
turned an accusing gaze on her husband. "Jimmy,
what have you been doing now?"

"Not guilty, my dear. I've no more idea than you
what's outside."

He had his suspicions as soon as the two young
men appeared with their burden. Junior brought
the screw driver, and a few minutes' work was
enough to change his suspicions to certainty, even

without the evidence contained in a square envelope, bearing Pollyanna's name.

"Jimmy," she almost shrieked, "it's from Uncle John. Another radio set."

"Yes, so I see. What confounded luck!" Jimmy looked highly annoyed. "I don't know whether I can exchange my set for something else or not."

"I won't let you try," Pollyanna declared. "Don't you see how perfectly it has worked out? Now Luke Geist can have a set, too. Oh, hasn't this been the most wonderful birthday!"

CHAPTER XI

SINCE Clifford's assistance was necessary for installing the new radio set in Luke Geist's room, Pollyanna found no difficulty in persuading Jimmy to let his assistant off for an afternoon. It is true that he remarked casually he supposed there was no hurry, but there was a twinkle in his eye as he said it. Knowing Pollyanna as he did, he was well aware that, from her standpoint, there was no time to lose.

Pollyanna did not disappoint him. "No hurry!" she repeated, indignantly. "No hurry, after that boy has been lying there all these years—"

"Kamerad!" Jimmy cried, holding his hands over his head, and Pollyanna, realizing that he had merely been teasing her to draw her out, laughed at her own vehemence.

They drove over to the Geist ranch the following day, and Pollyanna was disappointed to find Luke in his least agreeable mood. She had been to see him several times since their first meeting, and on the last visit she had been flattered by the certainty that

137

Luke was glad of her coming. But if he felt either pleasure or gratitude on the present occasion, he concealed his emotions admirably. His gruffness, as he acknowledged the introduction to Clifford, told Pollyanna what to expect. He refused to evince the slightest interest in the radio set, as she enthusiastically dwelt on its possibilities. She could see that Clifford was annoyed, and inclined to question the wisdom of bestowing so valuable a gift on so sullen a young man, too ignorant to appreciate what he was getting. It was when Clifford's back was turned, that Pollyanna caught a gleam in Luke's eyes which helped her to interpret his strange mood. To the young male of the species nothing could seem more humiliating than to lie there helpless before the eyes of a normal, vigorous young man. When Luke glared at Clifford as if he hated him, it only meant, Pollyanna was sure, hatred of the fate that had flung him sprawling there, as inert as a felled tree.

Caught between these masculine silences, the one of envy the other of disapproval, Pollyanna felt impelled to incessant chatter. She explained to Clifford that the cabinet must stand close by Luke's bed, where he could reach the dials easily, and she explained to Luke that she had brought a pair of ear phones in case he wished to listen in after the household had retired. "I remember your telling me once

that you were bothered by lying awake, and while
I'm not sure there is something on the air every hour
of the night, there's more than you would believe,
thanks to the differences in time."

Luke surveyed the ceiling in what seemed a bored
silence and Pollyanna noticed that Clifford's neck
turned a dark, angry red. "You used to sit up late,
hunting new stations, didn't you, Clifford?" she said,
determined that her companion should assist in the
conversation, besides performing the practical serv-
ice which was the excuse for his presence.

Clifford dropped his work instantly, and faced
about with the clearly defined intention of showing
this sulky brute on the bed how a fellow was supposed to act when a lady did him the honor to address
him.

"Why, yes, Mrs. Pendleton, I used to get a great
kick out of finding new stations. The fellows in our
office back East had a sort of rivalry to see who'd
get the most. I've sat up half the night, many a
time trying to get the stations on the Pacific coast.
Mother used to scold me regularly every morning.
Mother liked to listen to a good program, but she
didn't care whether the station was ten miles away
or a thousand."

"What was the most distant station you ever succeeded in getting?" demanded Pollyanna, more for

Luke's benefit than because she was especially interested.

"Well, I got England two or three times, and I picked up Buenos Aires once or twice one winter. And of course I got all the principal stations in this country."

Luke stared at him with an expression of angry incredulity. Pollyanna was sure that, with the absurd sensitiveness which is the hall-mark of ignorance, he suspected Clifford of making fun of him. She checked her impulse to explain. Luke would understand presently, and until he found out a few things for himself, it was probable that explanations were useless.

The work Clifford had come to do was finished at last. "I'll sit on the edge of the bed, if you don't mind," he said politely to Luke. "There's hardly room for a chair." He seated himself, and began turning the dials. Snatches of music, scraps of talk, disconnected as the errant thoughts that flash through the mind when one is falling asleep, sounded faintly in the small room. Then an announcer's voice broke out in a roar that made Luke jump, and suddenly a violin was playing a Chopin nocturne, the tones exquisitely soft, every note as distinct as if the artist stood beside them.

Mrs. Geist appeared suddenly in the doorway and

stood there agape. As the first notes sounded, Luke
had turned his head quickly. Now he lay without
stirring, his long unkempt hair streaming over the
pillow. His eyes were closed, Pollyanna noticed, but
she saw his lips trembling under the fuzz of neglected beard. She laid her hand on Clifford's arm,
the more easily to check him if he should start to
speak, but the young man, after a surprised glance at
her face, seemed to divine her wish and remained
silent.

The invisible musician played the selection
through, and then a man's voice in a conversational
tone announced the station and the musician's name.

Luke's eyes were opened widely now. As he
listened, he seemed to be holding his breath. Pollyanna said with affected carelessness: "Clifford,
hadn't you better show him how to tune in for himself?"

"Yes, but first he'd better put this station down so
he can get it another time. You see—" He hesitated a moment, then spoke the other's name—"You
see, Luke, the pointer on this left-hand dial is at
seventy-five, and on the right-hand dial, the pointer
is at sixty-nine. So any time you want this station,
put the pointers in the same position."

All Luke's surly indifference dropped from him
instantly. "You mean I can hear that again?"

"Why, not those particular selections, but anything the station happens to have on." Clifford was amazed that it should be necessary to give this explanation to any American adult, forgetting the years that Luke had been apart from the world. He went on hurriedly, "Now *you* try it. Take hold of the knobs this way, and when you hear something, turn first one and then the other till you find which way to turn to make the sound clearer. Now, go ahead. You can't hurt anything."

It was some minutes before Luke was successful. Then he turned a bewildered face toward them. "Sounds like talking," he said.

"Yes, they try to get as much variety as they can, talks and singing and church services and instrumental music, and all sorts of things. This is a talk on agriculture, I guess, and you've tuned in right in the middle."

Pollyanna studied Luke's face rather anxiously. He did not seem to be listening to the talk, but rather to be absorbed with some disquieting thoughts of his own. The speech came to an end in about five minutes, and the announcer spoke, giving the name of the station. Luke looked at Clifford as if he felt the need of an interpreter. "Where was that man talking?"

"In Cedar Rapids, Iowa."

"Say, you think you can kid me because I'm laid out here like a dead man. But above my chin, I'm as alive as anyone."

Clifford swallowed. "I don't wonder it's hard for you to take it in, old chap. It's as near a miracle as anything that ever happened, I guess. But just the same, that man was talking in Cedar Rapids, Iowa."

Luke looked almost fearfully toward the radio. "Then you can hear things all over—can't you?"

"Sure. You can hear a band concert in Washington, D. C., and in five minutes, be listening to Will Rogers in California. Sometimes just to show what they can do, I suppose, they'll have a nation-wide hook-up. Somebody in New Orleans will introduce a speaker in Chicago, and after he has finished, they'll switch you to New York, and back to Seattle, without losing a minute. Radio is really—"

Clifford stopped short. With a queer movement Luke had buried his face in his attenuated pillow— Pollyanna always longed to set fire to that pillow, and replace it with one from her own stores—and broke into agonized weeping.

Pollyanna looked at Clifford. Apparently the young man was waiting eagerly for his dismissal, for at once he rose to his feet and tiptoed from the room. Mrs. Geist had already vanished. Pollyanna waited patiently for the storm to subside.

After a rather long time, so long that she felt her own nerves getting on edge, Luke turned a wet, flushed face, and looked about him searchingly. Pollyanna knew by experience what he wanted. She fumbled hastily in her pocketbook, found her handkerchief and presented it to him. Absurdly inadequate as was the small embroidered square, it was distinctly better than nothing. Luke blew his nose echoingly, then lay back on his pillow and looked at her through reddened lids.

"Guess you think I ought to be wearing petticoats, and doing up my hair in curl papers."

Nothing is more scathing than the contempt of the helpless male for the weakness of women. Pollyanna knew this and hastened to relieve his mind by saying contemptuously, "What an absurd idea!" And this was no pretense. For all his hysterical weeping, there was nothing womanish about Luke Geist.

A little reassured by her vehemence, he went on to explain. "It kind of took me off my feet, you see. It came over me all at once, that lying here I could be listening to folks everywhere. When that fellow talked about hearing England, he wasn't lying, was he?"

"No, indeed. Of course that wouldn't often happen, but all real radio fans love to get distant stations. I'm more interested in what I hear than where it comes from."

Luke's gaze turned toward the cabinet beside his bed. "Say, that must have cost a lot of money."

"I don't know what it cost. You see I had two sets given me for my birthday, and, of course, no one could possibly need two."

"No, I reckon not. But look here, why should you give *me* the extra one?"

Pollyanna resolved on frankness. "I'll tell you, Luke. It seemed to me you'd get as much out of it as anyone I knew."

"I reckon you're right. I've nothing else to do, day or night." He looked hard at the instrument. "It's bound to be company," he said and she realized that he was trying to thank her, and was extremely embarrassed by the necessity of doing so.

She tried to relieve him by being very matter-of-fact. "Yes, it will be company, Luke. You'll find it interesting and amusing, but you'll be surprised how much you can learn."

"Learn? Well, what do I want to learn for?"

Pollyanna blinked. For a moment she had difficulty in believing him in earnest, and as if suspecting her incredulity, he continued in a raucous voice, "An education's going to do me a lot of good, isn't it?"

"Why, you're just the person who must have an education," Pollyanna retorted. "Your brain's as good as ever, and your chance lies in using it."

Luke's pallid face reddened violently. For a moment she was afraid he was going to cry again, but he only said savagely, "I'm not bragging about my brains, but if they were a lot better than they are, they wouldn't do me any good, unless I had legs to match 'em."

"Now, Luke, I'm going to tell you a story, a true story that will make you ashamed of that speech. It's about a man I heard of soon after the war. When he was a boy, he was caught in a terrible blizzard and almost frozen to death. They had to amputate both legs and one arm. They saved three fingers, as I remember it, on the other hand."

"Gosh, they didn't leave him much, I'll say. If I'd been him," commented Luke with savage sincerity, "I'd have thanked 'em to have finished up the job, and amputated my head."

"Well, he hadn't any parents, and it looked as if he'd have to live and die in the poorhouse. But somehow or other, he got the chance to lay his case before the town officials. He pointed out that if he got an education he would be able to support himself, and if he didn't get an education, he'd be a public charge as long as he lived. I don't know

whether it was the audacity or the logic of his plea
that won him supporters, but anyway, it was
arranged for him to go to school. He had never
had anything to speak of in the way of an education,
but you can imagine how he studied now. Well, he
went to college. By that time he was able to earn
a large part of his expenses—"

"Earn 'em!" Luke interrupted. "How in Sam
Hill could a fellow with nothing to work with but
three fingers, earn money to go through college on?"

"Three fingers and his brains," Pollyanna corrected him. "I don't know what he did, but it
doesn't matter, for if he couldn't have done one
thing, he'd have found another. That's where the
brains come in, you see."

"If you don't have hands and feet to help you,"
argued Luke, "I can't see how brains and an education can do much."

"Well, my answer to that is that they *did*. This
isn't a made-up story, Luke; it's true. He got
through college, and if I remember right, he became the editor of a small town newspaper, and made
a success of it. He was sent to the state legislature.
He became a prosperous, successful, influential man.
After the war, the Government brought him East,
to talk to the soldiers who had been badly mutilated.
You see by that time he had artificial limbs—two

legs and an arm—and he looked very much like other people. He has died since, and I'm sorry, for the world needs such object lessons."

Luke looked hard at her and suddenly he smiled. Pollyanna could not remember that she had ever seen Luke smile before, and she was astonished at the difference it made.

"You seem to have had a lot of unlucky friends." He was actually chuckling. "You're always telling me about somebody worse off than what I am. First it was that woman you said hadn't nothing but a brick wall to look at, lying on her back for twenty years."

He had remembered, then! Pollyanna was inordinately pleased.

"Yes, that woman was really a friend," she said. "The man I didn't know personally, but I know all about him. And what other people have done, you can do, Luke."

She found Clifford waiting for her alone. Mrs. Geist had disappeared in the mysterious fashion of which she had the secret, and at the sight of Pollyanna, Clifford's face showed relief. Though he had been touched when Luke broke down and wept, he felt that the Geist ranch was a rather sinister place, and that it would be a satisfaction to get away.

"You can't help being sorry," he told Pollyanna

as they drove homeward, "but he's the kind that makes you wish he was all right, so you could give him the kicking he deserves. The way he takes your kindness for granted, and acts as if he were doing you a favor by allowing you to present him with a handsome present, gets my goat. Honestly now, doesn't he sometimes make you feel as if you were casting your pearls before swine?"

Pollyanna answered with a cryptic smile. "I have an idea," she said, "that some day Luke will surprise us."

CHAPTER XII

AN UNANSWERED QUESTION

THE world so soon grows blasé regarding the miracles of science, that Pollyanna was delighted to find her neighbors as interested in her new radio set as if it were the only one of its kind. Pollyanna herself never lost her sense of wonder over the marvels of the age. An airplane flying overhead, the realization of man's most audacious dream, invariably caused a tingling sensation along her spine. Even a telephone seemed to her less a convenience than something out of Arabian Nights.

In this western community, where money was scarce and reserved strictly for the necessities of life, radio was almost as much a novelty as in the year of its invention, and everyone was excited at the prospect of finding out how much new truth there was in the stories told about it. All this was gratifying to Pollyanna. If people stopped her to make inquiries about her new possession, she was as voluble as if she had been promised a commission on all the sets she could sell. She not only invited all her acquaintances to come and hear her radio, but urged them to bring their friends. Jimmy wondered, rather uneasily, whether they would ever again have a quiet evening to themselves.

It did not occur to Pollyanna to question her own discretion till one evening about two weeks after her birthday. They had just finished supper when the Murrays' car, muddy and dilapidated, drove into the yard. Even after a protracted drought, the Murrays' car always looked as if it had made the trip through an uninterrupted succession of mud-puddles.

Pollyanna was reminded of the occasion when she had first made the acquaintance of the Murrays. Now, as then, there were five women in the car, and again old Mrs. Murray, Mattie's grandmother, had to be lifted and lowered to the ground like a piece of unwieldy luggage. As Pollyanna went to welcome her guests, she recognized the three Murrays and also Mrs. Dunn, who had been to the house a number of times to get books for herself and her daughter. The fifth was slow to leave the car, and Pollyanna did not recognize her.

She shook hands with Mattie, wondering what had happened to the girl to make her look so pale and worried. "You've come to hear my new radio, I know," she said. "I'm so glad to see you all." And then she turned toward the car where the one passenger remained, as if when it came to the point, her courage failed her. Pollyanna thought this very likely. The timidity of some of these ranch women wrung her heart. Apparently they saw so little of their kind that in the presence of a stranger, they were impelled to flight, like scared rabbits.

Mattie spoke and her voice was as tremulous as if she and Pollyanna had not sealed a pact of friendship long before. "Mrs. Pendleton, I want you to meet—"

The seated figure rose suddenly and emerged from the car. In contrast to Pollyanna's preconceived idea of shrinking timidity, her air of defiance was almost a shock. Pollyanna recognized her immediately. "Oh, Miss Walker and I have met before!" she exclaimed.

The girl spoke brusquely, disregarding the extended hand. "Mattie didn't ask me to come," she said. "I saw 'em driving by, and guessed where they were going, so I asked 'em to take me along. Folks said you were inviting every Tom, Dick and Harry, and I couldn't see why I didn't have as good a right as anybody else."

"Why, of course," cried Pollyanna. "You are very welcome." The girl's aggressiveness would have seemed amusing, had it not been for an uneasy apprehension in the back of her consciousness. Suppose Jerry should drop in? This undisciplined young

creature showed her emotions so unmistakably that
Pollyanna felt no little concern over the prospect
of having her in the same room with Dorothy and
Jerry. It might easily mean a disagreeable scene,
if nothing worse.

The company made their way to the house, allowing old Mrs. Murray to set the pace, and so moving
slowly. Pollyanna hoped that Dorothy, in view of
the fact that all the callers were women, might have
taken refuge upstairs, but when the delegation
entered the living-room, Dorothy, who had been sitting reading, rose to greet them. Pollyanna found
herself envying the girl's poise.

"Dorothy, I think you know most of these friends,
but I'm not sure you've met Miss Walker. Miss
Blythe, Miss Walker."

Dorothy's eyes scanned the group, seeking the
stranger, and came to rest on the flushed, defiant
girl. "Miss Walker," she repeated smilingly, and
nothing in her manner betrayed she had ever heard
the name before. But the sudden fire blazing in
Minnie's eyes should have enlightened her, Pollyanna thought.

As they took their seats, Minnie Walker chose a
chair next to the one Dorothy was occupying, and
even pulled it a little nearer to that of her rival. It
seemed to Pollyanna that Dorothy did not altogether

relish this proximity. There was a shade of uneasiness in her manner as she said, "I don't know why I should have the rocking-chair. Won't you take it, Mrs. Murray?"

The old woman shrilly professed her satisfaction with the chair she had chosen. "Rockin'-cheers is all right ef a body wants to go to sleep, but tonight I'm a-goin' to keep my eyes and ears open. I don't b'lieve half what folks tell me 'bout that new radio as they call it. I'm eighty past, and I haven't never heerd of sech goin's on, not sence I was born."

"There's always something new, isn't there?" Pollyanna said cheerfully. "I prophesy we'll make a radio fan of you before the evening's over. Here's Mr. Pendleton. He'll show you some things that will surprise you."

In the hour that followed, Pollyanna was increasingly aware of Minnie Walker's complete indifference to one of the most marvelous of twentieth century inventions. The radio set, unlike the children proud parents wish to exhibit to admiring visitors, conducted itself in the most exemplary fashion, and, by degrees, the incredulity of the listeners changed to delighted wonder. For once these ranch women forgot their reserve. They broke out in little cries. They chattered excitedly in the intervals when Jimmy was tuning in to new stations. But Minnie

Walker sat with her eyes on Dorothy, apparently oblivious to everything else in the room. Once or twice Dorothy turned and addressed her with some casual remark, to which the girl replied in a curt monosyllable.

A brass band in Denver was contributing to the entertainment of the group, and old Mrs. Murray's foot was tapping out the rhythm, when Minnie Walker rose, stepped close to Dorothy, and stooping, said something in her ear. Dorothy looked up with a start. From her post of observation on the other side of the room, Pollyanna thought she recognized a look like consternation on the face of her governess. But after a moment's hesitation, Dorothy, too, rose and crossed the room with a deliberation that seemed a challenge. She opened the door leading to the porch, and the two girls passed out of sight and hearing; and while Pollyanna accused herself of folly, she would have given much to have thought of a good excuse to follow them.

She might have been relieved by Dorothy's casual tone as she addressed her companion. "Does the radio bore you? It does lots of people, I know. I suppose we'll tire of it after we've had the set longer. But of course out here, away from everything—" she left the sentence unfinished, and said with a change of tone, "Sure this isn't too cool for you?"

Minnie ignored the inquiry. She leaned toward the other girl and spoke hoarsely. "I want to ask you a question."

"A question? Me?" Dorothy's pretense of surprise somehow seemed cheap, beside the other's terrible sincerity. "Of course, if there's anything—"

A hard voice interrupted ruthlessly. "What do you want of Jerry?"

"Of Jerry?" Dorothy repeated the name with an air of trying to gain time, then fell back on her dignity. "Why, really, I can't see how that is any concern of yours."

"Then I'll tell you," Minnie retorted. In the semidarkness of the porch, her eyes seemed fairly luminous. "It's my concern because I'm crazy about him. I care so much that I don't mind your sneering and laughing any more than so much wind in the trees."

"I really think," said Dorothy with the invincible hatred of plain speech, characteristic of her type, "that we'd better go into the house. It's much too cool out here," she added, with a desperate pretense at being casual.

"Answer my question first. What do you want with Jerry?"

"Even if you've lost your head about him, I don't see that you've any right to question me."

"Well, I've got the right, whether you see it or not. For he used to like me. I don't say he was wild about me, same as I am about him, but he liked me. There had been other girls, but he was done with 'em. He told me he was. And then *you* came."

Dorothy drew back. She had plenty of courage, but something in the way the girl spoke the last four words sent a chill to her heart.

"You turned his head. You was different from us girls here in the valley. You'd been to places, and you could talk about things we'd never heard of. It set him up to have you fall for him. Everybody was talking about it and that pleased him. Jerry wants folks to think he's a regular masher. He just swaggered when they teased him about you."

"Have you nearly finished?" Dorothy spoke wearily. "Mrs. Pendleton will think it very strange if we stay out here longer."

"I'm doing my share. I'm telling you things. Now you tell me. What do you want with Jerry? If you're crazy about him, same as I am, I haven't anything to say. You had a right to get him away from me, just as I have a right to get him away from you. But if it's just a game to you, if you're only playing with him, 'cause you like to see a man making a fool of himself about you, and girls making fools of themselves about him, I want to know it, that's all. And if that's it, I'll tell you right here that you're going to pay."

It was not quite easy for Dorothy to preserve her air of nonchalance. She had known, of course, that jilted girls were apt to be unreasonable and resentful, but they kept their feelings to themselves as well as they could. This fierce young woman who bared her emotions so ruthlessly was something new in her experience. Looking into those luminous, menacing eyes, Dorothy found herself shaken. She did not give the answer her rival demanded. Perhaps she could not, for the coquette uses her own heart for a counter in the game, as well as the hearts of others. She fell back upon evasion.

"I think this is quite enough melodrama over a simple, friendly acquaintance. I can't understand why a girl should wish to expose her feelings to a stranger, but the fact that you enjoy doing it, doesn't mean that it is necessary for me to do the same. And your being foolish about Jerry doesn't give you the right to catechise me."

She rose with dignity. Minnie Walker rose, too, but turned to the door that led outside. "Tell the folks I'll be waiting for 'em in the car," she said.

The girl who made a fetish of appearances uttered a shocked exclamation. "You can't do that."

"Why can't I?"

"What will your friends think? You drag me out here, and then you go off and sit by yourself in the dark. It will be perfectly plain to everyone what has happened. I should think you'd have more pride."

"Should you?" asked Minnie indifferently. "Well, there are some things I should have expected from you, but it seems they're not so."

She vanished in the darkness of the outside world, and Dorothy re-entered the house, making Minnie's excuses in a voice that gave the lie to every word she uttered. Miss Walker's head ached. She had thought it might help her to get out on the porch, but it didn't seem to do any good, and so she had decided to wait for them in the car. She had asked her to say goodnight to Mr. and Mrs. Pendleton, Dorothy offered as a final fabrication. She saw incredulity in the faces of the Murrays, anxiety under Polly-anna's pretense of sympathy, but to both she was indifferent. Something else was engrossing her attention.

What *was* it she wanted of Jerry? She only wished she knew.

CHAPTER XIII

A MORNING OF SURPRISES

POLLYANNA reproached herself that she had allowed so long a time to elapse without seeing Luke. The installation of a radio set in the room of the lonely invalid seemed to her a profoundly interesting experiment, and she had fully intended keeping in close touch with the unfortunate young man in order to test his reaction to the sudden widening of his horizon. But Judy, with that disregard of parental plans which characterizes the best regulated children, had developed a mysterious rash over night, and her mother, less inclined to take chances than when her tested physician was around the corner, promptly put the child to bed and forbade the others to come near her. Under these circumstances Judy required a surprising amount of entertainment, and Pollyanna's hands were full.

The rash proved nothing serious. After giving Pollyanna several anxious days and nights, it disappeared as mysteriously as it had come, and Judy, feeling extremely important after her brief quarantine, was allowed to join the family circle. For

the first time in a week, Pollyanna had leisure to
think of Luke Geist, and her reflections were unreasonably self-reproachful. Without wasting another hour, she backed the car out of the barn-garage,
invited Ruth and Jiggs to accompany her, and drove
to the Geist ranch.

Mrs. Geist was improving, Pollyanna told herself. She actually said good morning, and at the
sight of Jiggs, raised her hands and cried, "Lordy!"
It pleased Jiggs to take this as a compliment, and
he ran over to Mrs. Geist, and stood on his hind legs,
grinning at her, and wagging his tail. It was
impossible to doubt his friendliness, and Pollyanna
would have sworn that a glimmer of a smile crossed
the woman's face.

It was to be a morning of surprises. At the door
of Luke's room Pollyanna halted with the vague impression that the sagging bed had a new occupant.
The next moment she uttered a delighted exclamation. "Why, Luke! I didn't know you."

She was aware, of course, that Luke must shave
occasionally, as otherwise his beard would be even
longer. But she had never chanced to see him when
his face was not disfigured by a dark stubble, at
least a two weeks' growth. By a similar process of
reasoning, she had reached the conclusion that Luke's
hair must be cut now and then, in explanation of the

fact that it was not so long as an Indian's, but she had never seen him when it was not down on his neck, testifying by its unkemptness to his disquieting disregard for his personal appearance. But today Luke was freshly shaved, and his hair, though evidently it owed nothing to a barber, had been cropped close to his head. And Pollyanna was astonished to find him a good-looking young man.

Luke was gratified by her failure to recognize him. He grinned as he inquired, "Thought I had a visitor, did you?"

"I didn't have time to get as far as that, but I had to look twice to be sure it was you."

"How do you like my looks?"

"Oh! Very much," Pollyanna cried with enthusiasm. "Why, Luke, you are really handsome."

"Ma cut my hair," Luke explained. "She puts a bowl over your head, you know, and cuts all 'round it. But I did the shaving myself."

His pride in his achievement had its pathetic side. Pollyanna could not keep a little tremor from her voice as she applauded him with a "Splendid!"

"I'm going to shave every few days now," continued Luke, with an air of conscious virtue. "No need for a fellow to look like his grandad, just because he's on his back, is there now?"

Again Pollyanna agreed enthusiastically.

"Ain't so hard as you'd think," continued Luke, as if unwilling to accept undeserved praise. "Ma brought me a looking-glass, but it was pretty hard, looking into the glass and shaving, too, so I made up my mind I'd get along by feeling. Safety razors are great inventions, when you have to lie down to it." He waved his hand lightly, as if to indicate that he was done with the subject, and inquired, "Did you hear the President night before last?"

"I'm sorry to say we missed that," Pollyanna admitted. "I knew the President was going to speak, and, of course, I meant to hear him, but a new book came by mail that afternoon, and Mr. Pendleton and I got to reading and for once we forgot all about the radio."

"Well, you missed something, I'm telling you. That was a great speech. If he runs again, I'm going to vote for him, if I have to be carried to the polls, slung over somebody's back like a sack o' meal. And say, have you heard that fellow that tells you about the principal things that have happened in the week? He's got a lot of inside dope, and he makes things seem different from what the newspapers tell you."

The change in Luke had gone deeper, Pollyanna perceived, than the superficial differences involved in a clean shave and a hair-cut. "You're enjoying your radio, then?" she said, her pleasure showing in her voice.

"I'll tell the world I am. Why, Mrs. Pendleton, I didn't know there was so many things to learn about. And I've been wondering—"

"Yes," Pollyanna encouraged him, when the pause became so protracted as to convince her that he was trying to find courage to continue.

"I like the books you've brought me fine, but I was wondering if—well, what I mean is, I feel as if I wanted to learn something. I'd like some true books, if you've got any, about honest-to-goodness folks, and things that really happened. You get me, don't you?"

"Why, of course, Luke. I think it is a splendid idea. I've got some fine biographies, and two or three scientific books, written in a popular style, of course, and several histories. Oh, I can keep you busy for a long time with that sort of reading."

Jiggs thought it time he was receiving some attention. He jumped on Luke's bed, and came over for a closer examination of this young man whom he had only seen once before, and regarding whom he was still doubtful. He sniffed Luke critically, and finally sat down beside him, panting ostentatiously and offering his paw.

"That's politeness," Ruth interpreted. "Now you

must shake hands, too, 'cause Muvver says we mustn't let little dogs be politer than we are."

The pessimist who holds that everything pleasant must necessarily be of brief duration had the right of it on this particular occasion. Pollyanna had never enjoyed a call on Luke as much as on this morning, but her stay was to be cut short. For outside the window a voice called shrilly, "Mrs. Geist! Mrs. Geist!"

Luke started, turning his big eyes in Pollyanna's direction. "Who on earth is that?" he exclaimed.

"I don't know. Shall I go and see?"

"Mrs. Geist," the voice cried again, and Pollyanna realized it was not so much a call as a scream. But evidently the imperative summons had reached Mrs. Geist in the mysterious retreat where she disappeared when Pollyanna invaded the seclusion of her home, for almost immediately two voices blended in a confused medley of talk, the one voice hysterical and vehement, the other, low and monotonous. Pollyanna was just thinking that something out of the ordinary must have happened to draw Mrs. Geist into a real conversation, when the louder voice cried, "I'm going to ask Luke. Maybe he'll have heard."

This time Luke recognized the speaker. "Gosh," he said, "I believe it's Min Walker."

It was indeed Minnie. She rushed into the room, her manner so distraught that for an unhappy moment Pollyanna actually thought that the girl had lost her mind. Advancing on Luke, apparently unaware that he was not alone in the room, Minnie cried, "Have you heard about Jerry?"

"Jerry? What about Jerry? Haven't heard a thing."

Pollyanna did not know whether Minnie discovered her presence at that moment or not. In either case, she turned to her for the information Luke was unable to give. "Have you heard about Jerry?" she panted. "Did they say what was wrong?"

"No, I haven't heard anything," Pollyanna declared, as Luke had done. "Sit down, child, and try to talk calmly." She made a valiant attempt to act on her own counsel, but her heart was fluttering with vague fears.

"Tom Murray was by the house fifteen minutes ago, and he said they had taken Jerry to the hospital at Sprague. He didn't know what had happened to him, only just that they'd taken him to the hospital."

"Funny he knew that and didn't know why," Luke exclaimed.

"He said he had heard it from one of the men at the mines."

"Tom's considerable of a kidder," Luke reminded her. "He may have thought it was a good chance to get a rise out of you. It doesn't take much, you know, to get you stirred up where Jerry's concerned."

The girl protested. "Oh, he wasn't jollying. Anybody could tell he was in earnest." Her gaze came slowly around to Pollyanna. "I came here horseback," she explained, "but it would take all day to get to Sprague on that old mare. Drive me over, won't you?"

"To Sprague? Why, that must be all of thirty miles?"

"Forty," Luke corrected her from the bed.

"And it would be foolish, don't you see, my dear, to drive there without even knowing that this story is true. And if Jerry is ill, you might not be allowed to see him, even if you went over." The further possibility that Jerry might not care to see her, was present in Pollyanna's mind, but she tactfully forbore to mention it, though secretly hoping that it might occur to Minnie herself.

But apparently Minnie's mind was of the single-track variety. The only thing that mattered was reaching Jerry. "I've got to find out," she muttered.

"Maybe Mrs. Pendleton would drive you over to

Deer Creek," Luke suggested. "If anything's wrong with Jerry, everybody there will know it. Folks in Deer Creek most generally can tell you everything that has happened and quite a lot that hasn't."

"All right," said the girl sullenly. She looked at Pollyanna, not interrogatively this time but impatiently, as if wondering why she did not start. And to Pollyanna there seemed no alternative to making her farewells, and taking an immediate departure.

Once in the car, Ruth peered cautiously over her shoulder at the lowering face of the occupant of the rear seat. "She's a naughty girl, isn't she, Muvver?" she confided in an echoing whisper.

It was impossible to ignore the remark. Pollyanna said hastily, "Oh, no, she's not naughty. She feels bad about something."

"It's naughty to pout," Ruth insisted, and Pollyanna, finding it difficult to keep from smiling, looked back at Minnie in hopes that she, too, would see the humor of the situation. But nothing in Minnie's expression indicated that she had heard either Ruth's criticism or Pollyanna's defense. And Pollyanna gave her up, and drove on.

It proved unnecessary to reach Deer Creek to learn what had happened to Jerry. Five miles from the Geist ranch they met a farm wagon which halted

at their approach. The road was wide enough at
this point for two cars to pass without difficulty, and
Pollyanna assumed that the reason for the halt was
that somebody had news to tell. As she came abreast
the wagon, she, too, halted, and a woman with a
peculiarly zig-zag smile, due to the fact that seemingly every other tooth was missing, looked past her
at the girl in the rear seat.

"Well, Minnie, I guess that Fitzgerald boy won't
be botherin' you girls none for a while."

Pollyanna heard Minnie's answering gasp, and
realized that the girl was physically incapable of
speech. "What happened to him?" she demanded,
nerving herself to hear the worst. It was true that
the woman's facetious air was hardly consistent with
grim tidings, but she was so evidently enjoying
Minnie's distressed uncertainty, that Pollyanna suspected she was capable of finding amusement in disaster.

The woman was watching Minnie, even while she
replied to Pollyanna's question. "Thrown from his
horse, he was. He was always too uppity about his
ridin', that young flipperty-gibbet. Kind of a joke
his being pitched off, same as anybody who didn't
pretend to be a rider."

It was useless, Pollyanna realized to protest
against her informant's idea of a joke. Man, alone,

of earth's inhabitants laughs, and Pollyanna was
sometimes shocked to realize how much laughter is
sinister and cruel. She only said, "How badly was
he hurt?"

"His leg was broke, just below the knee. The
boys that was near him say that his horse stopped
pretty quick, and Fitzgerald started to jump up and
run after it. But, of course, he wasn't up to
runnin'."

The man beside her, silent up to this moment, gave
way to wheezy laughter.

"He's got pluck all right, that boy," he volunteered. "Two other cowboys was with him and they
came ridin' up, hell for leather. And Jerry says as
cool as a cucumber, 'Boys,' says he, 'up till now I've
been incog,' says he. 'Let me interduce you to His
Highness, the Prince o' Wales.' A broken leg ain't
no joke, I'm tellin' you. That boy's got pluck, all
right."

"Yes, I'm sure he has," Pollyanna agreed. "Do
you know whether the fracture was a serious one?"

Neither of the pair could give her any information
on that score. "They took him to the horspital at
Sprague," the woman said, "An' it's more'n likely
them doctors there'll cut off his leg."

"Oh, no," Pollyanna protested. "There wouldn't
be any reason for that, just a broken bone."

"I don't take no stock in horspitals nor doctors neither," the woman persisted. "They're always cuttin' folks open in horspitals and takin' out somethin' the Lord put in for some good purpose. And they don't think no more o' hewing off a leg or an arm than I would of steppin' on a potato bug."

Fearing that this conversation would not tend to quiet Minnie's taut nerves, Pollyanna thanked them, and started the car. But once safely past, she turned to interrogate Minnie. "Do you want to go back to Geist's, and get your horse, or shall I drive you home?"

The girl looked at her so dully that for a moment Pollyanna thought she had failed to understand the question. She was about to repeat it, when Minnie said abruptly, "I want to go to Sprague."

"I'm sorry, Minnie, but I can't take you to Sprague," Pollyanna spoke with a firmness intended to settle that question finally. "For one thing it would be too long a drive for me, and for another, I think you had better wait till you are sure Jerry is allowed to have callers."

Minnie Walker raised her angry eyes. "I'll bet you take the other girl over, that Blythe girl. She won't wait for an invitation. She'll want to go as soon as she hears he has been hurt."

This statement struck Pollyanna as so probable

that she took refuge in dignified silence. As the road widened a little at this point, she undertook to turn, and achieved the feat in course of time, though not till the perspiration stood in beads upon her forehead. Then again she addressed Minnie, "I'll drive you back to Geist's so you can get your horse. Of course, you can do as you please about going to Sprague. That isn't my concern. But I can't drive you there."

Minnie accepted her refusal in stony silence, and Pollyanna drove back over the route she had so lately traversed. Her strong sympathies made the trip a rather painful one. She was sorry for Jerry, sentenced to lie on his back for days and perhaps weeks to come. She was sorry for her silent passenger, whose love and pride were both scorpion-whips for her tormenting. And lastly, she was rather sorry for herself, though she did not attempt to define the latter emotion. She kept up an intermittent conversation with Ruth till the chimney of the Geist ranch house showed over the rise of the hill. Then Minnie spoke.

"I'll get out here," she said gruffly. "You needn't drive any further."

Pollyanna stopped obediently. Then as the girl alighted, the sight of her sullen, unhappy face wrung Pollyanna's heart. She leaned across Ruth's little body to speak to her. "Good-by, Minnie. I'm so sorry—for everything."

The girl muttered something that might have been a farewell, but certainly was not a "thank you," and trudged off through the dust. And as Pollyanna started the car, her feeling of being sorry for herself was suddenly clearly defined in her own mind. Hard as the day had been, the worst was yet to come. She must go home and break the news to Dorothy.

CHAPTER XIV

DOROTHY MAKES UP HER MIND

"SISTERS under their skin," said Pollyanna to herself after she had finished telling Dorothy of Jerry's accident. It was not an original remark, of course, but Pollyanna, unlike the majority of people, laid no claim to exceptional originality. Two girls could hardly be more striking contrasts than Dorothy and Minnie Walker, yet their reaction to this disturbing bit of news was almost identical. Dorothy had more self-control, of course, but while she listened without any great display of emotion, her first words showed that kinship to Minnie on which Pollyanna had mentally commented.

"How far is it to Sprague?"

"Too far to think of going there today," said Pollyanna with finality.

Dorothy gave her the benefit of a haughty stare. "I don't know what you mean."

"Well, I think you'd better wait a little. I said the same thing to Minnie Walker."

"Oh, that girl!" Dorothy's lip curled. "Of course

174

she'd want to rush over the minute she heard the news. Poor Jerry!"

"Well, she has known Jerry a long time, and perhaps she has as much right to hurry over to see him as you have. You're not engaged to Jerry, remember."

"If I'm not," returned Dorothy coldly, "it's not Jerry's fault."

"I suppose not. Well, be careful, my dear. Don't let your sympathy get the better of your common sense. Think it over for a day or two. Then if you must see Jerry, I'll go with you."

Apparently a day was as long a period of inaction as Dorothy could endure. When the following morning, she again spoke of driving to Sprague, Pollyanna offered no objections. The children were left in Nancy's care, and at ten o'clock, the two were on their way. Dorothy drove, and though the rough roads prevented rapid progress, they made better time than if Pollyanna had been at the wheel. They had brought their luncheon along, as well as some glasses of Nancy's jelly and a bag of oranges for Jerry, and on the outskirts of Sprague, they halted the car by the roadside and dispatched their makeshift meal. Dorothy professed to be nearly starved, though Pollyanna was inclined to regard her nervous onslaught on the sandwiches as a mere bluff.

The hospital at Sprague was a one-time boarding-house, partially remodelled, but still ugly and inconvenient. The former dining-room had become the men's ward, and here they found Jerry, one of a strange miscellany of patients. There were two Mexicans in the room, who having nearly killed each other in a fight over a woman, were now convalescing amicably in adjoining cots. Their heads rose from their pillows as Pollyanna and Dorothy entered, and so did the grizzly head of an old miner, who, as Pollyanna learned later, had missed great wealth by the narrowest of margins, and now was being cared for at the expense of the county. A man whose features proclaimed a mixture of Indian blood was not sufficiently interested to turn his head to look at them, and a similar indifference was noticeable in a bandaged individual, an Eastern tourist, whose car had skidded on a turn, and flung him over a precipice. In this heterogeneous assembly, Jerry, as Pollyanna noted regretfully, seemed handsomer and more appealing than ever.

The fact that they had driven more than forty miles for the sole purpose of seeing him failed to impress Jerry as worthy of comment. He greeted them hilariously, and not knowing his little joke had already gone the rounds, proceeded to give them the benefit of it.

"Ladies, I'm forced to confess that I've been incog since our acquaintance began.   Let me introduce you to His Royal Highness, the Prince of Wales. You'll excuse me for not getting chairs for you.   Oh, Nurse! Hi there, Nurse!"

A pretty young woman, with a distinctly proprietary manner, came into the room.   "Now you mustn't go to shouting and getting yourself excited," she reproved him.

"Nurse, I want some chairs for my friends, that's all.   Meet Mrs. Pendleton and Miss Blythe.   And this, ladies, is the ministering angel of the County Hospital, as well as the sunshine of Paradise Alley."

"You certainly are one to talk," said the girl, dimpling over the compliment, nevertheless.   "I'll get some chairs"   She brought them and added in a tone of authority, "You'd better not stay too long today.   The fracture is doing nicely, but it is better for him to keep pretty quiet."

Pollyanna had been taken aback by finding Jerry a ward patient, but almost at once she decided that this was a reason for congratulation.   It was impossible to indulge in any sentiment while every man in the ward lay gazing in the direction of Jerry, all straining their ears to hear every syllable that was spoken.   Pollyanna, looking about her, saw an odd anticipation on each face, as if they had been an audience at a play, waiting for the curtain to rise. And it seemed to her that in the attentive regard of one or two, she saw a certain satisfaction, as if they recognized in this debonair cowboy a champion who would avenge the wrongs they personally had suffered at the hands of women.

If Jerry had his moments of depression, he showed none of it on this occasion. He described his accident with humorous exaggeration, and laughed the more loudly when he saw the tears in Dorothy's eyes. He told funny stories. He bragged in his customary, rather endearing fashion. When presented with the oranges and jelly, he insisted that the fruit should be passed to every patient in the ward and even the Indian unbent at this attention. On the whole the young man had never seemed more attractive, and Pollyanna was thankful that so many eyes were riveted on him and his companions. Dorothy might proclaim her entire indifference to public opinion, yet Pollyanna felt her incapable of making love before an audience.

At the end of half an hour, the nurse appeared, and looked at them significantly. "Is it time for us to go?" Pollyanna asked, as a mere matter of form, for the girl's manner had answered the question before it was put into words.

"Well, it won't do for him to get excited," the

nurse replied. "He's doing so well that we don't want complications." She took his pulse and frowned. "It's faster than it was this morning," she announced, with an air of displeasure.

"That's because you're holding my hand, Nurse," Jerry explained, and the ward tittered. The fresh color deepened in the girl's cheeks, but she only smiled disdainfully. "You've been talking too much. That is what's the matter," she retorted. "All this visiting's hard on you."

Pollyanna wondered what was covered by the phrase, "All this visiting," and concluded that they were not the first callers. She rose obediently, and Dorothy, with a tight-lipped smile that only partly concealed her displeasure, followed her example. The leave-taking was extremely matter-of-fact, thanks to the presence of the nurse, who stood guard as if defying anyone to agitate her patient by a display of affection. And during their farewells, Dorothy became a trifle more reserved than before. The other men in the ward looked vaguely disappointed as if they had hoped for at least a kiss at parting.

Dorothy was very quiet as they started for home, and Pollyanna tried to encourage her. "It looks to me as if Jerry were getting along nicely."

"Why shouldn't he? What's a broken bone to a healthy, young man?"

"Well, it oughtn't to be serious, of course. I was delighted to find him in such good spirits."

"That's part of his courage," Dorothy said sharply. "One couldn't be really in good spirits in that horrible place."

"Oh, did you feel that way about it?"

"How could I help it! All that riffraff, listening to every word we said. And that insufferable girl!"

"I admit the patients were a rather miscellaneous crowd. But Jerry is such a sociable creature, I'm not sure he would be contented in a private room."

The car slowed down a little. "Mrs. Pendleton," Dorothy said in a resolute voice. "I've made up my mind."

"Oh!" Pollyanna was conscious of a sense of chill. "Do you mean—"

"Yes, I'm going to marry Jerry."

Pollyanna sighed. "I was afraid this would be too much for you."

"It isn't. It's not that at all. But I know my own mind at last."

"It's a serious decision, Dorothy. Of course love is the most important thing. I admit that. But there are so many things to be taken into consideration, tastes, ideals and—"

"Nothing makes any difference," Dorothy broke in. "He's the man I want."

"Well, dear, I hope you'll be happy," said Pollyanna, sighing again. "I feel terribly responsible.
Now if it were Clifford, I'd be perfectly satisfied."

The girl laughed with unexpected gaiety. "Poor
Clifford! He's a nice boy, but don't you see, Mrs.
Pendleton, that he'd make a sort of standardized
husband?"

"Standardized?"

"Yes, all the virtues catalogued. Everything
women want in husbands. Specially prepared for
the June trade, don't you know. No surprises! No
romance!"

"If you mean by a standardized husband a good
man you can count on in every emergency, that's the
kind I have, and I thank God for it."

"Oh, Mr. Pendleton's a perfect dear," Dorothy
admitted, and to Pollyanna's sensitive ear there
seemed a suggestion of patronage in the appraisal.
"And I'm sure you're as happy a woman as I've
ever known. But, Mrs. Pendleton, I think I'd get
rather bored with that comfortable, easy-going happiness. I want a little uncertainty, a few thrills. I
want excitement, if you know what I mean."

"I know what you mean well enough!" retorted
Pollyanna, who always resented the condescension
of that overworked phrase. "All I can say is, that
I don't believe you. I don't believe there is a girl

anywhere who is such an idiot that she won't be satisfied with happiness."

"Of course you're not very old, Mrs. Pendleton, but after all, we belong to different generations, don't we, and the new generation has a rather different point of view. You don't have to tell me that things won't be as peaceful with Jerry and me, as they are with you and your husband. I expect we'll quarrel terribly and there'll be times when we won't understand each other a bit, and sometimes we'll both feel as if we were walking on the edge of a precipice. But there's something about that which appeals to me. It's life. I wouldn't like anything too cut-and-dried."

"Well, Dorothy Blythe, I think you are talking nonsense," Pollyanna exclaimed. "I don't believe you are speaking for your generation, or for yourself either. It's just that you don't know what you're saying. If thrills are the most desirable thing, then life on a roller coaster would be the ideal existence."

"But there you would know what to expect, so that would grow tiresome," laughed Dorothy.

"Not always. Sometimes there is an accident on a roller coaster," Pollyanna reminded her grimly. "And everything smashes." She realized that she was growing irritated, and that it would be better to talk of something else. Was the younger generation always like this, she wondered, so sure of itself, and patronizingly superior, when experience protested. Standardized husbands, indeed! And then realizing that this epithet was really responsible for her feeling of ill-temper, Pollyanna laughed at herself. Jimmy only grinned when he heard how Dorothy had classified him. "Well, there won't be any monotony in their establishment, if this match ever comes off."

"I'm afraid there is no escape," Pollyanna said dolefully. "She says she has made up her mind, and I believe she has, and, of course, Jerry has been wild about her from the first."

"Well, for Clifford's sake, I'm glad to have it settled," Jimmy declared. "Clifford's too good a chap for a flirt to keep dangling indefinitely. I'm afraid he'll take it hard, but the sooner he knows, the better. Clifford deserves a different sort of wife—somebody more like you, honey."

Poor Dorothy and her silly talk of thrills! Pollyanna felt a sudden pity for the girl. If after a dozen years of married life, her husband should say a thing like this to her—say it with a look in his eyes which showed he meant every word—that would be a thrill worth having.

CHAPTER XV

MATTIE BRINGS GOOD NEWS

WHEN on the following Saturday, Dorothy asked if she might have the car for a few hours, Pollyanna did not counter by inquiring her destination. Neither did she offer to accompany her. In spite of her deceptive little girl appearance, Dorothy was a woman, with the right to choose for herself, however disastrous the consequences.

"Of course you may use the car, Dorothy. I shan't want it today."

"I won't be gone any longer than I can help," the girl said, her color rising. "But at best, it'll take some time."

"Don't hurry, Dorothy. As far as that's concerned, you don't have enough time away from your responsibilities."

Though Pollyanna spoke so lightly, something in her expression must have betrayed her secret uneasiness, for unexpectedly two arms went around her neck and she felt herself violently kissed. "Don't look so solemn, dear Mrs. Pendleton," a voice im-

plored. "After all, every girl has to find happiness
in her own way, doesn't she?"

"Yes, my dear. I only hope it will prove to be
happiness," Pollyanna answered, and wondered at
her own lugubrious tone. But when half an hour
later, she watched Dorothy drive away, she realized
that her foreboding had not communicated itself to
the girl, for Dorothy's face was radiantly expectant.

Pollyanna's feeling of depression was not relieved
when Clifford turned up about the middle of the
afternoon. She was out in the yard giving attention to her neglected garden, when the young man
joined her, and he affected the greatest interest in
Puck's growth, and Pluto's tricks, and Jiggs' latest
exhibition of intelligence. Being more or less
familiar with the methods of young men in love,
Pollyanna accepted this display of enthusiasm for
what it was worth, and waited for the inevitable
question.

It came in course of time. "Is Dorothy anywhere
around, Mrs. Pendleton?"

Decidedly it was not going to be an easy afternoon. While Pollyanna had not been commissioned
to enlighten Clifford Wright as to the state of Dorothy's affections, she was determined to have no hand
in keeping him in ignorance. She said quietly,
"Dorothy has driven over to Sprague. You have

heard of Jerry's accident, of course. He is in the hospital there and this morning she went to see him."

The young man's ingenuous face clouded over. "I wish she wouldn't do that!" he exclaimed. "Of course she does it out of the kindness of her heart, Mrs. Pendleton, but people here are likely to misunderstand her."

"I think they are likely to understand her perfectly, Clifford."

The young fellow looked puzzled. "Oh, no, Mrs. Pendleton, they'll think she has a crush on the fellow, instead of just pitying him, and wanting to help him."

Pollyanna was silent, but again her expressive face spoke for her, and even Clifford had no difficulty in interpreting her look.

"Why, Mrs. Pendleton, you act as if—you can't mean—"

"I'm afraid I do, Clifford."

"But really Mrs. Pendleton, you're all wrong there," Clifford exclaimed. "I understand just how Dorothy feels about Jerry. She's sorry for him, you know. She thinks he might have been quite a man, if he'd had early opportunities. There's really a good deal to the fellow, and she'd like to help him as much as possible. But those folks around here aren't capable of understanding a generous friendship like that.   And if she drives over to Sprague to see him, they'll think she is like the other silly girls who run after Jerry."

It really was too bad of Dorothy.   Pollyanna's sense of exasperation reddened her cheeks becomingly.   Clifford having concluded his impassioned defense, looked at her for corroboration, and seemed disappointed when she remained silent.

"You see, don't you, Mrs. Pendleton—how she—"

"No, Clifford," Pollyanna said firmly.   "I don't agree with you.   The fact is that Dorothy doesn't talk that way to me."

"But, Mrs. Pendleton, you can't imagine her falling in love with that fellow!   Why, he's a bounder. If she married him—But she couldn't marry him. It's an insult to her to think of such a thing."

Under its coat of tan, Clifford's face had gone white.   Between her sympathy for him, and indignation with her governess, Pollyanna was having a hard time.   Yet the sooner Clifford knew the truth, the easier it would be for all concerned.   She said quietly, "Clifford, it doesn't matter what I think. Dorothy is the one to settle the question, and I advise you to have a frank talk with her and know just where you stand."

"You mustn't suppose, Mrs. Pendleton, that Doro-

thy hasn't been straight with me," exclaimed the
young man, whose great anxiety, apparently, was
that the object of his affection should be misjudged.
"She's never given me any reason to think she could
ever be anything to me but a friend. And that's
more than I have a right to expect," he went on
humbly, "a wonderful girl like that. Why, I'm not
in the same class with Dorothy, and I know it, but
alongside that cowboy I'm an ace."

This expression of self-esteem, as near boasting
as anything of which Clifford was capable, closed
the conversation, for at that moment, Dorothy drove
into the yard. She alighted rather languidly, but as
she approached the two in the garden, her manner
changed to mild enthusiasm. "Clifford!" she cried.
"Isn't this nice!"

Pollyanna cut her raptures short. "How's
Jerry?"

For a perceptible instant, Dorothy hesitated.
Pollyanna was sure she was tempted to deny having seen Jerry, and regretfully resisted the impulse.
She answered carelessly, "Oh, I guess he's doing
well. I only saw him a moment." The implication
was that Jerry had been a secondary consideration
in her trip to Sprague.

Pollyanna felt herself on the verge of a quarrel.
It was a relief to have the Murray car approach

with Mattie as the sole occupant. The girl climbed
out, encumbered with a heavy package of books,
and at once Dorothy was on her feet.

"Oh, there's Mattie Murray, looking for another
thriller. I'll attend to her, Mrs. Pendleton."

"No, thank you, Dorothy." Pollyanna made the
negative a trifle more emphatic than the "thank
you." "I'll attend to Mattie, and you can entertain
Clifford." She marched away without looking back,
hoping that what she had said to the young man
would give him courage to demand an accounting.
But from what she knew of Clifford, she suspected
that if Dorothy was reluctant to discuss the situation, he would not insist on it.

It was a relief to turn from Dorothy's love affairs to the less hectic interests of Mattie Murray.
Mattie looked a different girl, Pollyanna thought,
from the shy, awkward young creature who had
accompanied the group of older women on the mem-
orable tour of inspection, which had been the start-
ing-point for so many worth-while things. Pollyanna reflected that if she had given Mattie a new
interest in life, Mattie had done as much for her.
It was really her success with the circulating library,
and her ambition to lessen the tragedy of Luke's
existence and to aid Mattie's passion for self-im-
provement, that had made Pollyanna's Western so-

journ not so much an endurance test as a glad adventure.

This afternoon the sight of Mattie's smiling face was balm to Pollyanna's mood. She put her hand lightly on the girl's shoulder, and kissed her. "Bless your heart!" she said. "This is like having a visit from a sunbeam."

Mattie gave a little excited laugh. "Mrs. Pendleton, I believe that game of yours is magic—indeed I do. Ever since you started me playing it, the nicest things have kept happening."

"They always do," laughed Pollyanna.

"They're not so much to tell about," Mattie explained, "only they give you a nice feeling. I was saying to Luke—Oh, you never told Luke about the Glad Game, did you, Mrs. Pendleton?"

"No, I never did," Pollyanna replied, surprised by the question. She would have thought it almost unsafe to introduce that subject in the little room where Luke lay helpless.

"Well, the other day Mother sent me to Mrs. Geist's on an errand. She was away when I got there, but Luke said she'd be back any minute, and so we just talked. And right off we started talking about you."

"Dear me, this *is* exciting," Pollyanna exclaimed. "I wonder my ears didn't burn."

"Well, if either of your ears burned, it should have been the right one, for we said the nicest things. Luke started it. He said he didn't believe there was anybody like you in the world. He said sometimes he lies awake nights trying to figure out what made you so much nicer than other folks."

"Perhaps you'd better not tell me anything more, Mattie," Pollyanna interrupted, "It might turn my head." As a matter of fact, this sweeping compliment from Luke Geist, of all people, gave her a rather absurd sense of having won a victory.

But Mattie did not take her protest seriously, for she continued serenely, "Well, I said I didn't know all the reasons, but I guessed I knew one, so I told him about the Glad Game. It's funny you never thought of telling him, Mrs. Pendleton, because he needs it worse than 'most anybody."

"I would have said he wasn't quite ready for it," Pollyanna replied, and mentally reproached herself for a lack of faith which apparently had meant a lost opportunity.

"Well, I told him, and first he said he couldn't play that game for sour apples. And then he laughed, and said—well, anyway, he had something to look at besides a brick wall. And then he told me about the sick woman who was a friend of yours— I guess you know who I mean."

"Yes," said Pollyanna. Not for worlds would she have let Mattie know how near the tears were at that moment.

"And then he said his legs might just as well be cut off, for all the good they were to him, but he s'posed he could be glad he had ten fingers. When he said that he laughed so hard he 'most scared me, because Luke never used to laugh. I thought maybe he was going nutty, you know. But he said you'd told him about a man who didn't have but three fingers—was that so, or was he joking?"

"No, that was true." And Pollyanna herself laughed, and thereby lightened the tension.

"And then he kept on, and said he was glad of his radio and 'specially the ear phones. He said he didn't mind lying awake hardly a bit now. And then he said the queerest thing of all, that if anything had to happen to him, he was glad it happened to his legs, instead of his brains. And we got so interested thinking up things, that by the time Mrs. Geist got home, I'd forgotten all about my errand and didn't remember it for the longest while."

Pollyanna was inclined to think the forgotten errand of slight importance, compared with what Mattie had accomplished, but guessing that this view might be considered heterodox in the Murray family, she discreetly kept her opinion to herself. And by this time, Mattie was ready to tackle the task of selecting new books for readers scattered the length of her homeward route.

"I've got a lot of books to change today, Mrs. Dunn's and Dora's and Mrs. Peterson's and Emily McIntyre's and our three. And Luke says that book about Andrew Jackson was worth all the made-up stories he'd ever read."

"I thought he would enjoy that," Pollyanna said. "And here's another just as good."

Selecting books for the various families on her list always fascinated Pollyanna. There were so many things to remember. Mrs. McIntyre, for example, had warned her not to send anything exciting, since books of this sort gave Emily the nightmare, and resulted in her rousing the household at two o'clock in the morning with cries of "Murder!" The popular Western yarns were rather unpopular in the valley, Pollyanna found. Only two or three readers, including Mattie and her brother, read them with enjoyment. All the others seemed anxious to prove that the author "didn't know what he was talking about."

"Here's a lovely detective story for Mrs. Peterson," Pollyanna said to Mattie, who joined in her chuckle. Mrs. Peterson was one of the house-keep-ers whose work is never done. Pollyanna had seldom been more thrilled than when Mrs. Dunn told her of calling on Mrs. Peterson at eleven o'clock one forenoon, and finding her absorbed in a book, while her unwashed dishes stood on the table beside her.

"It honestly scared me," Mrs. Dunn confessed. "There was her kitchen same as when the folks went to work in the morning, not a stroke o' work done, and they'd be coming home for dinner in an hour. 'For goodness sake, Mrs. Peterson,' I says to her, 'have you gone plumb crazy? Your men won't have nothing to eat—nor nothing to eat it out of,' I says, meaning the dishes. And she looks up at me wild-eyed and says, 'I've got to find out who killed that old man.' If I hadn't been there to hustle her along, there'd have been trouble in the Peterson family." Pollyanna had enjoyed the story hugely, and hoped that other housewives in the valley might occasionally forget the monotonous grind of their daily toil in vicarious flights of imagination.

The books were ready at last, and Mattie rose reluctantly to go. At the door she paused to say, "Luke wants me to come over every Tuesday evening that I can get away. There's something on the radio at eight o'clock he thinks I'd like. Luke's having so much company nowadays that Mrs. Geist doesn't hardly know what to do."

"Does she listen in at all, I wonder?"

"Yes, indeed. She thinks she'll peel her potatoes or do her mending in Luke's room, so as to hear what's going on, but she gets so interested that she forgets all about what she is doing. The other day she let a big kettle of potatoes roll right off her lap, and she had to get a broom to poke 'em out from under Luke's bed and the dresser. Luke laughed so when he told me. Doesn't Luke laugh a lot now, Mrs. Pendleton?"

Pollyanna was laughing too, as she waved good-by to Mattie. Then catching sight of Dorothy, sitting all by herself on the porch, her face very grave, Pollyanna asked anxiously, "Where's Clifford? I supposed, of course, he was going to stay to supper."

"Why, he happened to think he must have some new neckties, so he drove over to Deer Creek. Poor Clifford!" Dorothy cried. "Think of depending on Deer Creek for neckties!" She laughed with a convincing air of merriment, but Pollyanna had her doubts.

CHAPTER XVI

A VIGIL

WHEN Pollyanna waked about two o'clock the following morning, her first thought was that she must be running a temperature. Then she recalled the reassuring fact that there had been ham for dinner, and that she had eaten rather heartily. Although reassuring, the recollection was not altogether satisfactory. It needed to be supplemented by a glass of water.

Pollyanna was sleeping on the porch, snuggled under heavy blankets, for though the late summer days were warm, sunset called for roaring fires, and the chill of the nights suggested frost. Pollyanna's reluctance to leave her bed, when balanced against her annoying thirst, seemed likely to tip the scale. She turned on her pillow and shut her eyes, resolving to drink her fill in the morning.

But thirst is one of the sensations difficult to ignore. Pollyanna's drowsy thoughts revolved like squirrels in a cage around cool, delicious drinks. Her imagination pictured a tall tumbler of iced tea, a slice of lemon swimming in the amber fluid, the ice tinkling musically against the glass. And then magically, the tumbler was filled not with tea, but with lemonade, and the pungent odor of the lemon, reaching her nostrils in a realistic whiff, rendered sound sleep impossible. And finally her over-active fancy simulated the sound of running water. She heard it splashing on stones, singing to itself as it rushed to its mating with an unknown lover. She found herself sitting up in bed, wetting her dry lips.

"I might as well have it over with," Pollyanna cried. "I can't possibly go to sleep till I've had a drink. Let this be a warning against over-indulgence in ham, except in the middle of the day."

Of course her warm bath robe and bedroom slippers were near, for the mother of three children can never count on an uninterrupted night's sleep, and donning them, Pollyanna wondered that she had been so loath to leave her bed. She made her way around the house to the kitchen door, left unlocked at night, according to the custom of the country. Thanks to the moonlight it was unnecessary to light a candle in order to find the water-pail. But with water at her lips disappointment awaited her. Thirsty as she was, Pollyanna was fastidious, too. The water came from the well deliciously cool and sparkling, but this had been pumped the night before, and had been standing in a warm kitchen.

Pollyanna tasted it hopefully at first, then critically, and finally with a shudder of repulsion.

"One thing's certain, I can't be dying of thirst," Pollyanna reflected, "because when people are in that condition, they'll drink out of mud puddles, and think it is perfect. I suppose as long as I'm wide-awake, I might as well go the whole figure, and have a real luxurious cold drink."

They kept two water-pails in the kitchen, and emptying the contents of one into the other, that none of the precious fluid might be wasted, Pollyanna went across the yard to the pump, leaving the kitchen door ajar. The moon was full and under its silver light, she found her way as easily as if it had been mid-day. Far in the distance a coyote yapped shrilly and an owl uttered its raucous cry, as if according to some pre-arranged signal.

Pollyanna reached the pump and filled her pail, and without waiting to return to the house, drank thirstily from the dipper kept for convenience's sake at the well. Then she retraced her steps to the kitchen, anticipating, now that her thirst was relieved, the luxury of her warm bed.

She set her full pail by the sink, and was turning to close the kitchen door, when a sound in the room attracted her attention. She turned her head, and for a moment was tempted to believe herself the

victim of a grotesque illusion. The moonlight
streaming through the window, revealed two animals, apparently at play, in the vicinity of Nancy's
rocking chair. They were about the size of cats,
and not unlike them in appearance, but country-bred
Pollyanna recognized them immediately. They were
skunks. Two skunks had taken possession of her
kitchen.

Pollyanna's arm extended in the direction of the
door, dropped noiselessly to her side. It was clearly
useless to remain standing, as if the new occupants
of the kitchen were gorgons with the ability to turn
the beholder to stone. Pollyanna subsided into a
chair, which, as good luck would have it, happened
to be ready to receive her.

Though she would have said she had not made a
sound, something attracted the attention of her un-
welcome visitors. They showed no signs of fear,
to be sure, but became alert, ready for action if
necessary. And then as Pollyanna remained motionless, hardly daring to breathe, they evidently
reached the conclusion that there was no occasion
for uneasiness, and resumed their investigations.

It was not Pollyanna's way to borrow trouble,
but on this unwonted occasion there were so many
disagreeable possibilities that it was out of the question to ignore them. Suppose Jiggs, who slept at

the foot of Junior's bed, should wake and with the uncanny intuition of something wrong, characterizing most dogs which are family pets, should come in search of her. At the thought of the possible consequences, Pollyanna with difficulty suppressed a groan.

Jimmy was not so likely as Jiggs to wake, but even Jimmy might rouse sufficiently to realize that his wife was absenting herself an unreasonably long time. Or one of the children might cry. Or Dorothy might be thirsty, as Pollyanna had been, and come downstairs for water. If any of these things happened, the playful animals which had taken possession of her kitchen, would in all probability fall back on the method of defense by which nature had fitted them for defying the teeth and claws of predatory beasts. Through the generations they had learned how little they had to fear, and in this strange environment their dominant emotion was curiosity. As they peered behind the brooms which Nancy kept standing in a corner of the room, or crawled under the kitchen cabinet, they showed as little timidity as if they knew themselves invincible.

Pollyanna sitting with strained immobility, as if she were taking part in a tableau, and the curtain was about to rise, found a new ground for apprehension. She realized she was not dressed for the

occasion. It was true that her bedroom slippers
were a warm, comfortable pair, which Nancy had
knitted for her, but though her bath robe was a
substantial garment, her bare ankles, showing above
the slippers and below the enveloping robe, assured
her that the night was cold. Entering by the open
door, a playful breeze fluttered the blue and white
cloth on the kitchen table, rattled the shades, frol-
icked with the blue and white curtains, and gave a
flattering share of attention to Pollyanna's ankles.
To sit quiet and contract pneumonia would perhaps
be more disastrous than the catastrophe which would
result if she rushed from the room, leaving the intruders to do their worst. But when it came to the
point, Pollyanna found herself incapable of stirring.
After all, pneumonia seemed a rather remote con-
tingency. She might get off with a cold in her head.

People talked of time flying, Pollyanna recalled
with a peculiar sense of irritation. It was true that
sometimes she felt that way herself, on a busy morning, when she had to stop work several times to
bind up Ruth's cut finger, sew a button missing from
Junior's second-best coat, or settle a dispute between
Junior and Judy. After a morning of these trivial
interruptions, Pollyanna could never believe her
ears when the clock struck twelve. But at present
the moments limped by on leaden feet.

She had heard the clock strike two just as she had left her bed, and when the musical note that meant the half hour reached her ears, she seemed to herself to have been sitting there, chilled, anxious and afraid to move, a long, long time. From that till three seemed such an 'endless interval that she made up her mind that the clock had stopped, and could hardly believe her ears again, when three silvery peals broke the quiet of the night. And then there was another long, chilly, disheartening wait, before the half hour struck again.

The moon had gone down by now. In the dark she could hear faint rustlings, audible footsteps of tiny feet, scratching sounds as if strong claws were testing some unfamiliar material. Perhaps even more harrowing were the periods of absolute silence, when Pollyanna sat with her hands clenched, nerved against something startling, like hearing the animals at play under her chair. "If that happens," Pollyanna told herself, "I know I'll scream, I just can't help it."

She was aware all at once that the darkness was less profound. She could again distinguish the familiar objects in the kitchen, the table, the rocking chair, the square outlines of the range. She could distinguish, too, objects less familiar, though she had seen enough of them to satisfy her for the re-

mainder of her life, two striped animals, not unlike
black and white cats, sitting quietly under the edge
of the table, as if a somewhat exciting evening had
been too much for them.

It was after four, and the room was filled with a
wan, sickly light, as if the ghost of a dead day had
entered, when Pollyanna suddenly faced the omi-
nous certainty that she was going to sneeze. The
strange thing was that it had not happened earlier,
but apparently delay had only rendered the impulse
more irresistible. Pollyanna pressed her shaking
hand against her upper lip. She set her teeth, defying a sound to escape them. She fought the sneeze
as desperately as if she had reason to know that
it would prove fatal.

But it was not for nothing that the breeze from
the mountains had fanned her ankles. The sneeze
would not be gainsaid. It escaped her at last, tamed
somewhat from its original exuberance, but a lusty
sneeze, nevertheless, and was immediately followed
by another, a counterpart of the original. With the
third sneeze, Pollyanna gave herself up for lost.

At the third sneeze the animals under the table
stirred slightly, and evidently one or the other expressed the opinion that they really should be going.
Unhurried, moving with a sort of swaggering defiance, they made for the open door, their luxuriant

tails erect. They passed so near Pollyanna that she could easily have put out her foot and touched them, though needless to say she ventured no such liberty.

Out on the porch they lingered, as though loath to say good-by to their kind hostess. The sky was paling in the East, and against it a fir stood tall and black, as if done in India ink. The growing light bespoke to other nocturnal creatures the need of haste, but the two skunks went their leisurely way, knowing they had nothing to fear.

Perhaps the most exasperating feature of that exasperating experience was the way Jimmy took Pollyanna's story. Of course Jimmy needed his sleep, but Pollyanna felt it absolutely essential to confide her adventure to sympathetic ears without delay. Under these circumstances, it was disappointing to have Jimmy casually advise her to go to sleep again. "You've been dreaming, dear," he explained kindly.

"Dreaming! Jimmy Pendleton, don't you suppose I know when I'm awake? I've been sitting there in the kitchen with the door open, till I'm almost frozen. See how cold my fingers are."

"By Jove, you *are* cold," Jimmy exclaimed. "Wonder if you could have been walking in your sleep. Because you know, Pollyanna, two skunks couldn't possibly have taken possession of our kitchen, and stayed on there for hours. Nobody ever heard of such a thing."

"Well, if nobody ever did, I've made an important contribution to natural science," Pollyanna declared, "because that's exactly what happened. And if I'd let a timber wolf or a mountain lion into the house, I wouldn't have been half as frightened."

Although Pollyanna's vigil did not result in an attack of pneumonia, as she had gloomily anticipated, nor even in a severe cold, it was some time before she recovered from its effects. For many weeks thereafter, she never opened an outside door after dark without peering apprehensively into the blackness. But apparently her nocturnal visitors, as well as she, had had enough of it, for never again, during her sojourn in the West, did she so much as catch a glimpse of those unpopular little animals, to whom the old French chronicler—impelled doubtless by some experience, even more harrowing than her own—gave the name, "Children of the Devil."

CHAPTER XVII

THE DANCE AT DEER CREEK

JERRY'S convalescence was rather slower than Pollyanna had anticipated, and every week during his stay at the hospital, Dorothy asked with a peculiar blending of shyness and audacity, if it would be convenient to let her have the car. It was not always convenient, as she must have known, but nevertheless she got the car when she asked for it.

"If she's really in love with him, think how hard it must be to have him in a hospital forty miles away," Pollyanna said to Jimmy. "Think how I'd feel if it were you, and I could see you once only a week."

Jimmy was unsympathetic. "It's a question with me," he replied, "whether that girl could really be in love with anyone. She's a glutton for admiration. She's like the head-hunters, except that she specializes in hearts instead of heads. But I can't imagine her feeling any unselfish affection for anybody."

Pollyanna thought him too severe. "You don't see her when she comes back from a trip to Sprague.

206

She's perfectly radiant, in spite of the fact that they have to do their love-making with an audience hanging on every word, and with a nurse standing guard to see that the patient doesn't get excited. It's a test of devotion if there ever was one."

It was August when Dorothy told Pollyanna that Jerry was leaving the hospital that week. And it was so clear that this announcement was a preliminary to one she considered of equal or greater importance, that Pollyanna found herself waiting rather breathlessly for the sequel.

"He's going to stay in Sprague till he feels up to riding again," Dorothy explained casually, "and when he comes back, they are going to give a dance for him at Deer Creek."

"A dance!" exclaimed Pollyanna. "That's a strange idea, it seems to me, when the poor boy's just able to walk."

"It isn't likely that we'll—" Dorothy was beginning, and then she checked herself, and rather self-consciously changed the form of her statement. "I don't imagine he'll dance all night, the way others do. These dances, Jerry says, begin about half-past eight, and last till five or six in the morning."

"And then they start the day's work, I suppose," commented Pollyanna absent-mindedly. She was thinking of the significant change in the pronoun.

"Are you going to the dance, Dorothy?" she asked bluntly.

"Why, yes, I think so. Jerry is very anxious to have me there," explained Dorothy, with a significant smile. "And he hopes you and Mr. Pendleton will come. It's a community affair, you see. There aren't any invitations. The women provide the refreshments, and the men chip in to pay for the hall and the music. I really believe you'd enjoy it for the novelty of the thing, anyway. Of course I want to go, since it is in honor of Jerry."

"I suppose so," said Pollyanna, and forthwith made up her mind to attend. But when she reported the conversation to Jimmy, casually mentioning her decision, even her complaisant husband protested.

"My word, Pollyanna, if that's your idea of a festive time, sitting up all night to watch a country dance—"

"Of course we won't stay all night, Jimmy. But I think it is up to us to attend. It looks to me as if Dorothy and Jerry would practically announce their engagement that evening. And as long as we're responsible—"

"Say, I like that!"

"Well, if we hadn't come West, Dorothy would never have met Jerry, so we're partly responsible,

even if we don't approve. In a sense we stand in
the place of her parents—"

"Worse and worse," Jimmy scolded. "I'll go to
the dance, if you think it is necessary because we
pay Dorothy a salary, but I'll be jiggered if I'll be
regarded as the parent of a girl old enough to be
married. If you keep on at this rate, in a week or
two you'll have me a doddering grandsire. It's
time for me to make a stand."

Pollyanna's suspicion that Dorothy regarded the
forthcoming dance at Deer Creek as an event of
supreme importance was confirmed by the discovery
that the young woman felt she had nothing fit to
wear on that occasion. She sent an order, special
delivery, to a big department store in a neighboring
state, and on the arrival of the material, set herself
to make a new frock in the height of fashion. Dorothy could have made a living anywhere as a dress-
maker. If her needlework fell below the standards
Aunt Polly had inculcated in Pollyanna, she had a
knack with draperies, which reduced Pollyanna to
speechless admiration. The georgette was flame
color, and the little frock, when Dorothy finished
it, would have held its own in more exclusive assem-
blies than Deer Creek was likely to furnish.

Pollyanna seldom questioned Jimmy's judgment
so much as on the day of the dance, when he re-

turned from work, bringing Clifford Wright with him. "Cliff is going to the shindig tonight," he explained. "And I told him he might as well go with us, and spend the night here."

"How nice," Pollyanna said diplomatically, and forced herself to smile. Of course it was always nice to have Clifford, but if the four of them attended the dance together, it would look as if Clifford were Dorothy's escort, and naturally Jerry would not like it.

"Is Jerry coming here for you?" she asked Dorothy hopefully.

Dorothy hesitated. "Do you know, Mrs. Pendleton, I'm wondering about it. He didn't say anything definite, but he may have thought I'd take it for granted."

"I see."

"And on the other hand, he may have taken it for granted I'd go with you. Of course, he hasn't a car and no very good way of taking me."

"If he comes, he'll be pretty sure to come early," said Pollyanna. "We won't be in any hurry to start." She still felt uneasy. It was true that Jerry had never seemed jealous of Clifford, but that was due, she felt sure, to his self-confidence. He was certain that in comparison with his splendid self, Clifford wouldn't have a chance.

Dorothy took her time about dressing, and when she came downstairs, oddly enough it was Jimmy who exclaimed. While liking Dorothy well enough, Jimmy had never been able to discover what it was in her that attracted other men. Pollyanna was secretly rejoiced that the slender figure in flame color had, at last, made an impression on her matter-of-fact husband.

"By Jove, Dorothy," he cried, "you're certainly out for a record tonight. The girls who don't want to lose their young men had better lock them up." But as he complimented her, the gravity of his expression contradicted the lightness of his speech. To him, as to Pollyanna herself, it seemed a tragedy that this girl should join her fortunes to those of that irresponsible dare-devil, Jerry.

"Half-past eight, isn't it?" said Dorothy, looking at the clock. "We'd better start. They'll have begun dancing by now and I'm sure—" She did not finish her sentence, but Pollyanna knew intuitively she had been on the point of saying that Jerry would expect her to dance the first dance with him. She glanced at Clifford, as he crossed the room to help the girl on with her coat and his unconscious look of adoration wrung her heart.

"Oh, dear," Pollyanna thought, "Why did things have to get so mixed up?" She sighed heavily.

"What's the matter? Doesn't sound as if you were in a festive mood. If you'd rather stay at home—"

Pollyanna shook her finger at him. "What a thoughtful husband," she mocked. "Ready to give up an evening's pleasure because his wife is tired." And then with a change of tone, "No, Jimmy Pendleton, you can't get out of it that way."

The dance was to be held in the nondescript building where a movie was shown once a month or so, and where during political campaigns, the voters gathered to hear reasons for voting for one or the other of rival candidates. Occasionally, too, a patent medicine vendor hired the ramshackle building for an entertainment, interspersed with laudations of some magic oil or miraculous pill. It looked a firetrap, and Pollyanna wondered that its rare periods of usefulness were assumed to justify its continued existence.

When the Pendletons' car stopped at the door, the sounds of merriment within the building indicated that the dance was under way, even though a surprising number of unattached young men stood around the door, both in the hall and outside, smoking and saying little.

As they entered the hall, Pollyanna looked around for Jerry. Several couples were dancing to music

furnished by an orchestra consisting of two violins
and a saxophone, all apparently self-taught, but for
the time being, most of these present were on-look-
ers. A group of scattered young women, corre-
sponding to the young men gathered about the door,
stood at some distance from these ungallant swains,
and talked with an abandon intended to indicate that
they were totally indifferent to the dancing. A few
girls, franker than the others, were dancing together, pretending to enjoy it as much as if provided
with partners of the opposite sex.

Pollyanna's eyes made the circuit of the room,
and came back to Dorothy. "I can't see Jerry anywhere," she whispered.

"Oh, he's not here, yet," Dorothy whispered back.
"If he were, he'd come to us right away."

"He couldn't if he were dancing, but I don't see
him on the floor."

A little smile flickered across Dorothy's face. "I
don't believe he would dance till we came," she replied, and Pollyanna nodded understandingly.

The dancers were exacting. When the music
stopped, there was an outburst of applause, an im-
patient protest against a moment's respite. Indulgently the players swung without delay into a
new selection. "Shall we try it, Dorothy?" Clifford
asked, looking down on the girl at Pollyanna's side.

Dorothy hesitated, and Pollyanna feared she was about to refuse. But possibly she was irritated by Jerry's tardiness, for she finally answered with a little laugh, "Why not? But I must get rid of my coat first."

"We'll take that, Dorothy," said Pollyanna. "There doesn't seem to be a coat-room." She waited till Dorothy had slipped out of her coat and into Clifford's arms, and then led the way toward the unoccupied benches, stopping several times to shake hands with some acquaintance, and introduce Jimmy.

The dance was far more interesting to watch, Pollyanna decided, than any other she had ever attended, and paradoxically, the people who were not dancing were as interesting as any. Grey-haired men and women were much in evidence, and so were children so small that as they sat watching the frivolities of their elders, their short legs extended straight in front of them. Some of them stretched on an unoccupied settee, were slumbering as peacefully as if they were in their own beds.

Over in one corner was the refreshment table, showing that the dancers would not lack sustenance to enable them to carry out their strenuous program. There were mounds of sandwiches, several baked hams, and baskets of cake and doughnuts. The smell of coffee was already contending with the

odor of tobacco, and some of the older men, Pollyanna noticed, had begun to munch sandwiches, as if
this bountiful table in the corner were the lure which
had brought them so far from home.

Mattie Murray ran up to her, radiating a delight
that was the most satisfactory of welcomes. "Oh,
Mrs. Pendleton, I didn't know you were coming."

"I wasn't really expecting to see you either,
Mattie."

"We're all here, Grandmother and all. Grandmother brings the rest of us, I guess. She
won't ever miss a dance. When she was a girl,"
explained Mattie with a touching faith in the rem-
iniscence of the older generation, not always characterizing modern youth, "she was a great belle.
It kind of disappoints her that the boys aren't fight-
ing one another to dance with me."

"You look very sweet tonight, Mattie. I can't
think your grandmother ever looked nicer when she
was a girl." Pollyanna had already been impressed
by the adaptability of the sex to which she belonged.
Though the older women were for the most part
dressed as decorously as if for church, the girls,
almost without exception, wore at least an apology
for evening dress, and looked not unlike girls at-
tending a dance in any part of the country. Among
the men, on the contrary, there was the greatest

possible variety of costume, except that the conventional evening clothes nowhere appeared. The majority wore business suits, though a number of the dancers had laid aside coat and vest. There were cowboys in chaps and spurs, and one blonde giant who wore overalls did not seem to lack attractive partners.

Mattie blushed with pleasure at Pollyanna's compliment, though an instinctive honesty led her to say, "You've seen this dress before, Mrs. Pendleton."

"Oh, I think not."

"Yes'm. It was the white one I wore to your house that night. I dyed it pink, and then I ripped out the sleeves, and turned in the neck. To-morrow," explained Mattie, "I'll sew the sleeves in again."

Clifford, who had yielded Dorothy to young Hale, came up at this moment and asked Mattie to dance. At once the girl was overwhelmed by shyness. Blushing crimson, she looked at Pollyanna, as if to ask her counsel in this unprecedented situation. And when reassured by Pollyanna's smile, she moved away with Clifford, her expression suggested not so much pleasure as an agonized determination to be worthy of the honor conferred on her.

When Clifford reappeared again and took up his

stand beside Pollyanna's chair, he consulted his
watch. "Why, Mrs. Pendleton," he exclaimed, "it
is ten o'clock!"

"Is it really?" Pollyanna felt a pang of uneasiness which Clifford immediately put into words.

"It's funny about Jerry's not showing up, considering that this affair is a sort of welcome home
to him—at least, that's what I understood."

"He hasn't been out of the hospital long," Pollyanna replied. "I hope nothing has gone wrong with
that broken leg." She leaned forward. "Why,
that's Minnie Walker, isn't it? Dear me! If she
talks as she looks, I'm afraid her partner isn't having a happy time." There was indeed, something
almost grotesque in the grim unresponsiveness of the
girl's face, as she danced past them. It occurred
to Pollyanna that probably she had come hoping
for a dance with Jerry, and that disappointment at
his failure to appear was responsible for her expression.

The noise in the room was now almost deafening.
The young country folks, a little shy and constrained
at first, had gradually thrown off their inhibitions,
and were shouting to be heard above the blare of
the saxophone and the screaming violins. Clifford,
again dancing with Dorothy, tried to say something
to her, stooping till his lips almost brushed her ear,

but she shook her head laughingly, putting her fingers to her lips, to suggest the uselessness of attempting a conversation.

Suddenly the room stilled, save for the noise of the instruments and the shuffling of feet. Some of the dancers stood motionless. All eyes turned to the door, which had swung open to admit two resplendent figures. There was Jerry, in the magnificent chaps he had worn to Pollyanna's dinner, and beside him, clinging to his arm and challenging the admiration of the assembly with a dazzling smile, was a girl whose pretty face was somehow familiar.

In an instant Pollyanna knew, and she caught Jimmy's arm. "It's the nurse, Jimmy," she gasped, "the nurse in the hospital."

Before Jimmy could reply, pandemonium broke loose. The assembly charged down on Jerry. The music stopped, and such was the tumult, that no one knew the difference.

Pollyanna caught sight of Minnie Walker, holding her partner back from the rush. The girl's face had undergone an extraordinary change. The sullenness, which to Pollyanna seemed her characteristic expression, had altogether disappeared. Perhaps the discovery that another girl had been subjected to the same humiliation as herself had proved oddly consoling. She looked amazed, but no longer as if she had a grudge against the human race. And when her gaze fell on Dorothy, who likewise was resisting the rush in Jerry's direction, the emotion rippling across her face seemed an understanding sympathy.

Dorothy crossed to Pollyanna. "Quite exciting," was her comment. "It shows how popular Jerry is, doesn't it?" She was smiling gallantly, but the face above the flame-colored frock was of a chalky whiteness.

Over the tumult of voices, Jerry shouted directions to the musicians and they started in valiantly, striving to be heard above the din. The dancing began again, and as the encircling crowd melted away, Jerry seized his companion, and swung into the crowded floor. Taking her cue from Dorothy, Pollyanna spoke casually.

"You young folks had better go on and dance your fill," she said, "for I warn you I have had almost enough of this."

Clifford looked at Dorothy inquiringly, then put his arm about her and swept her into the throng of dancers. And, as luck would have it, within two minutes they were shoulder to shoulder with Jerry and his partner. Dorothy twisted her head, looked over her shoulder, and smiled. Jerry grinned back, nothing in his manner suggesting that he was anything but pleased with himself.

They got away before midnight, and the coolness of the fresh, outdoor air after the close atmosphere of the hall, the quiet after the uproar, seemed like relief from pain. Dorothy and Pollyanna occupied the rear seat of the car, and the girl, huddling into the corner, closed her eyes and sat without speaking. Pollyanna longed to put her arms about her and give voice to the sympathy that tore her heart, but instead, she, too, sat without speaking throughout the drive.

The house was very still. Jiggs, sleeping at the foot of Junior's bed, rose to challenge their entrance. Then recognizing his mistress, he wagged his tail and lay down again. A lamp had been left burning in the living-room, mutely welcomng them home. There had been a fire in the fireplace, but only a few glowing coals were left.

Dorothy, her eyes very brilliant in the pale oval of her face, bade Jimmy and Pollyanna good night, and then turned to Clifford. "Thank you very much, Cliff," she said.

"Thank me for what?" the young fellow questioned, with an uneasy laugh. "I'm the grateful one."

"Thank you for saving me from humiliation,"

the girl said steadily. "You see I was jilted to-
night, Clifford. I really thought Jerry and I were
engaged. He's been making love to me almost
ever since I came here, and after his accident, I
found I cared for him,—and told him so. And
then to-night—of course, you can't save me from
the shame of it, and the hurt of it, but you did
keep people from being sure that he had just thrown
me over."

Clifford uttered an angry exclamation. "I'll find
that hound and horsewhip him, if I get six months
in jail for it."

"Of course you'll do nothing of the sort," said
Dorothy. "That would only tell people what I
don't want them to know. Funny I should care
about what those people think, isn't it? But it seems
as if I couldn't bear to have them laughing at me
or pitying me. At the same time, I thank you for
wanting to hurt him."

She lifted her face, kissed him gently on the
cheek, and went out of the room, leaving three
people temporarily incapable of speech. And Pollyanna saw that Clifford's eyes were brimming with
tears.

CHAPTER XVIII

BACK TO NATURE

POLLYANNA had made up her mind that the family should take a holiday. In the winter looming ahead, there would be little chance to vary the monotonous routine, but the perfection of the late summer days imperatively clamored to be utilized in some festive fashion. When Pollyanna said as much to Jimmy, he smiled in the knowing way characteristic of husbands who are sure they know all that is passing in the minds of their wives.

"What you really mean, my dear, is that our governess, having been jilted, needs something to divert her thoughts from that painful experience."

"We all need diversion," said Pollyanna. "You need to think of something besides dams, and I need a change myself. Then the children have studied all summer, not hard, of course, but regularly, and they deserve a holiday."

Jimmy started, of course, by regretting that it would be impossible for him to get away, but Pollyanna had expected this, and continued to question him as to the sort of outing he would prefer. And

when she broached the subject to Clifford, she
found him an invaluable ally. "Of course the chief
needs a holiday," said Clifford, "and you see that
he takes it." Not content with this support, he
began to tell thrilling stories of the fishing back
in the mountain sections, and Jimmy listened with
an interest that rejoiced Pollyanna's heart.

Since constant dripping can wear away stone, it
is not strange that incessant reiteration of an idea
has an effect on the strongest will. And so it came
to pass that one bright morning the Pendletons were
preparing for a week in the mountains. Arthur
Hale was to accompany them, and Mattie Murray
was coming over to keep Nancy company. The
first stage of the journey they were to make in a
farm wagon, borrowed from Mr. Schroeder, then
they and their belongings were to be transferred to
saddle horses and pack animals. Jimmy, in khaki,
with a revolver stuck in his belt, looked surprisingly
like the Captain Pendleton who had impressed Pollyanna as such a resplendent being when he returned
from overseas.

Jimmy had been a little in doubt about taking
Ruth, but Pollyanna insisted that her youngest would
prove as good a pioneer as any in the company. It
was bad enough to leave Jiggs behind. Had they
been able to make the entire trip in the farm wagon,

she would have taken him along, but Jiggs was neither capable of riding horseback, nor of climbing mountain trails. He knew from the beginning that he was to be left at home, and he had been sulky and abstracted in consequence. Pollyanna petted him outrageously during her week of preparation, in hopes of assuaging the hurt to his pride, but without success.

They shut him into the living-room the morning they were to leave, and Jiggs stood on his hind legs, and from the window watched them load their stuff aboard the wagon. His expression was divided between anguish and cynicism, as if he were now forced to believe the worst of human beings, though it broke his heart. Junior's spirits were clouded by his pet's dejection. "Please, can't we take Jiggsy, Mother?"

"Darling, we couldn't. Jiggs wouldn't be equal to a trip like this. You know how tired he gets on the walks you children take. He's much better off at home."

"I wish he wouldn't look so sad," Junior sighed, "for it makes me feel as if I wouldn't have a good time myself."

Up to the moment of departure, Jiggs preserved a dignified silence. But when the wagon creaked out of the yard, his emotions overcame him, and he howled shrilly. Pollyanna patted her son's shoulder, but even as she saw him struggling with his tears, she knew that the novelty of the trip would soon erase the memory of that reproachful face, looking from the living-room window.

The first day they traveled by the farm wagon till they reached the spot where all roads ended. There was a camp at this point, with half a dozen wagons and cars standing about, and as many camp fires lighted. Here they met the man whom Hale had engaged to bring horses and burros suited for the trail. Pollyanna surveyed the restless broncos uneasily.

"Are you sure they're gentle, Arthur? For you see none of us are used to this sort of riding, and the children——"

"Now don't you worry, Mrs. Pendleton," Hale said with decision. "You won't, any of you, have anything to do but sit quiet on their backs. They'll attend to the rest."

The women slept that night in the farm wagon, while the men, including Junior, rolled up in blankets and lay beside the fire. "You'll feel stiff in the morning," Hale admitted, "But tomorrow night, believe me, you'll have as comfortable a bed as you ever slept on." Pollyanna recalled that cheering promise as she lay on the bottom of the wagon, atop the hay which was to be fed to the horses in the morning, trying vainly to go to sleep. Yet it was not altogether the hardness of her bed that accounted for her wakefulness. It was the strangeness of everything, the flickering of the scattered fires, the neighing of the horses, the audible snoring of a camper sleeping fifty feet away, the occasional barking of a dog. It was even strange to look up and see the stars.

She went to sleep at last and waked refreshed, after she had, as she told Jimmy, "straightened out the kinks." The children and Dorothy were conscious of no kinks, and Pollyanna, who could never realize that she was any older than when she was married, was forced to admit that youth is something apart from spirit. Arthur had insisted on getting breakfast, and a huge pot of coffee was sending out its fragrant invitation. Of course they had slept in the clothes they had worn the previous day, so that making one's toilet was reduced to a minimum. Those who were sufficiently squeamish to care for washing their faces and hands went down to the brook to do it.

Pollyanna had been amazed by Hale's estimate of the amount of provisions they would need. "Why, Arthur," she expostulated, "we couldn't eat that in a month!"

"Oh, couldn't we! Wait! Wait till you've been out all day in that mountain air, and see what you can eat. Of course we'll catch plenty of trout, but you can't live on trout and nothing else, and I don't want to come home early, because the provisions have run out."

"Neither do I," acknowledged Pollyanna. "It doesn't seem possible we can dispose of such quantities, but, of course, we must be on the safe side."

This conversation occurred to her as she sat on the ground and ate her breakfast. There were bacon and eggs, baked beans, thick slices of bread and butter, and coffee. Pollyanna protested when Arthur handed her a piled plate, but to her astonishment, she found herself clearing it without the least difficulty.

"We'd better eat plenty," Arthur told them, "because we'll have a cold snack in the middle of the day. But to-night we'll have a dinner that'll be a dinner. You see if it isn't."

Though they had risen with the birds, it was some time before they were ready to start, for the loading of the pack animals was not only a work requiring skill and patience, but one that also required time. The man who had brought the horses had spent the night, and lent his skilled assistance, while Jimmy did his best and kept his eyes open. It was necessary that the pack should be perfectly balanced, not too heavy for the animal's strength, but not light enough to encourage a frivolous spirit. The knots must be secure, for if anything slipped, disaster would ensue. As one after another of the animals was loaded and tethered, Pollyanna found difficulty in concealing her amusement. "The idea of our needing all this stuff," she said to herself. "Arthur must think we have the appetites of farm hands."

The packs were not all food of course. A certain number of pots and kettles, of shining tin plates, and equally shining tin mugs, of simple tools like axes and spades, and an extravagant quantity of blankets, made up the load of the patient animals, but it was with the supply of provisions that Pollyanna especially quarreled. She had catered for the group—with the exception of Arthur himself— and wondered who was expected to dispose of those potatoes and boxes of canned goods, of that bacon and fruit and butter and sugar. She felt sure they would bring home at least one half of what they had taken.

They were ready at last and started up the trail, Jimmy leading, with Ruth on the saddle in front of him. Junior and Judy came next, looking a little frightened, but very important on their wiry little

ponies. Dorothy followed, very trim in her khaki
suit with its divided skirt. Then came Pollyanna,
and behind her the pack animals, with Arthur bringing up the rear.

Overhead the sky was cloudless. Wild blackberry
vines grew near the trail, laden with late berries
which looked appetizing, Pollyanna thought, even
if she had so recently finished her breakfast.

It was not for long that they kept this orderly
line of march unchanged. Soon Jimmy had dismounted, and was walking beside the horse, his
arm about Ruth to steady her in the saddle. Arthur, too, dismounted, and somehow managed to
keep up with the procession and yet pick quantities
of delicious blackberries. Pollyanna felt that she
would never again eat blackberries, without recalling the invigorating air, the sound of hoofs clicking
against stones, the heat of the warm sun, and the
nearness of the sky.

The trail began unassumingly with a modest
slope, and thick woods on either hand. But after
an hour, they came to sharp pitches, which the animals climbed with protesting grunts, and abrupt
declivities where Pollyanna felt that her horse was
shutting itself up like a jack-knife. She had to set
her teeth to keep from shrieking cautions to the
children, to Jimmy, to everybody, but set her teeth

she did, and never once did she cry, "Be careful!"
Personally, she was inclined to think that her self-
control entitled her to a Carnegie medal for hero-
ism, but since she was the only mother in the company, she realized that no one else could guess
what her silence cost her.

After a time there were no friendly woods flank-
ing the line of march, but a steep wall on one side
of the trail, and a sheer precipice on the other.
Again Pollyanna longed to utter warnings, and
again forced herself to remain silent. It must be
safe, since Arthur, strolling just behind her, was
whistling cheerily, but she wondered what perver-
sity in the four-footed kept those horses on the
danger-side of the path. Was there, even among
them, the mock courage which prides itself on taking risks?

The party took a good hour for luncheon, for
though the meal was soon dispatched, the horses
needed rest. Clifford had been better than his word.
He had put up their lunch separately, so as not
to disturb the packs, and there was plenty of bread
and butter, sliced ham, wedges of cheese, and
oranges, the latter seeming as out of place on this
mountain trail as a bath tub. There was water
in thermos bottles, no surplus, but enough. Pollyanna could have eaten more, but at the same time

it was good to move about, to admire the landscape, and to feel Ruth's little hand in hers.

"The horsies look cross," Ruth commented, pointing to the animals who stood with drooping heads and their feet wide apart.

"Poor things, I don't wonder," said Pollyanna. "We've been riding all the way up, and they've had to climb and carry such heavy loads. Think how tired they must be."

"I'm tired, too," Ruth said and rubbed her pink knees. "Aren't you glad, Muvver, you haven't four legs to get tired, the way a horsie has?"

After luncheon, their time of climbing was short. They reached the peak of their journey and began the descent toward the plateau, where they were to make their camp. Pollyanna found the downward march more trying than the upward climbing. She had no idea that an ordinary horse, making its way down a mountain trail, could twist its body into such extraordinary contortions. Sometimes when the animal was negotiating an especially deep descent, she felt certain she would pitch over its ears, and not stop for a thousand feet or so. Owing to the preoccupation due to these emotions, she failed to notice the scenery and suddenly found herself convinced that their little caravan had entered the Garden of Eden.

The trail had ended in a broad, level valley encircled by mountains. At some distance flowed a stream which must have found an outlet, not visible to them, between two of the guardian peaks. Against the massiveness of the mountains, rocky and formidable, the valley with the luxuriant grass and countless evergreens, seemed of unearthly beauty.

Pollyanna's enthusiasm lasted till she found the caravan moving briskly in the direction of the river. "Oh, Arthur," she cried protestingly, "we're not going to cross, are we?"

"Sure thing."

"But, Arthur, I'm sure there'll be nice camping places on this side."

"You just leave it to me, Mrs. Pendleton," said the young man briskly. "And don't you worry a bit. This river has quite a current, but it's not at all deep. Why, even our packs won't get wet."

Pollyanna subsided, even checking an almost irresistible impulse to beg the children not to fall off. And Arthur's optimistic prophecy was fulfilled to the letter. The procession crossed the river in a zigzag line, halted occasionally when some of the thirsty brutes decided it was an ideal time to take a drink. But once on the other side, they moved with weary deliberation, following Arthur, as he led the way to the camping place he had selected.

"Arthur, this is ideal!" Pollyanna cried. And even Dorothy, dropping the listlessness which had characterized her ever since the night of the dance, echoed her approval.

The site was a little higher than the surrounding land and dotted with noble spruce trees. Fifty feet away a fall of water, pitching itself recklessly from the top of a tall cliff, formed a tumultuous brook, hurrying with a musical babble, to join the river they had just crossed. Arthur called their attention to this with as much pride as if it had been his own invention.

"You need good water near a camp, you know. This is as cold as ice. Fed from the snow back in the mountains. Now after we get the packs off these burros the next thing is to make our beds. I promised you a good one, and it'll be good, but it will take some time to make it.

After the tired horses and donkeys were picketed and cropping the fresh grass with relish, they began on the work of preparing a luxurious camp bed. Small spruces were cut down, the ranger carefully selecting those which had no chance for symmetrical development. At first the pile of boughs, six feet square, looked anything but inviting, but when it had been built up some two feet, Arthur changed his tactics. Breaking off the soft, new growths of the spruce, he thrust them into the foundation, so that they stood upright.

"That's all," he explained. "We'll build it up this way for another two feet, and if it isn't the best bed you ever slept on, I'll eat it, branches and all."

Ruth opened her eyes at this reckless promise. "Is you a horsie?" she demanded.

"We can finish this now you've showed us how," said Pollyanna, without waiting for an answer to her small daughter's question. "And you can make *your* bed."

"Yes, let's make ours," said Junior who had been watching the process with great interest.

"Oh, our bed won't amount to much, son," Arthur gravely assured him. "Men can sleep on 'most anything and not mind, but ladies' bones are soft." However, at Pollyanna's protest, he cut down a few of the unwanted trees and arranged them to make a second bed, smaller than the first, since it was to be occupied by three people instead of four.

The question of the camp-fire came next. There was no need to sacrifice any growing thing for fire-wood, since everywhere were fallen trees or limbs broken off in some winter storm. Arthur and Jimmy, between them, dragged into camp the

bleached skeleton of some giant, which for centuries had stood guard on this slope, succumbing
at last to the weakness of old age. It was hollow,
seemingly, to the top and Arthur piled wood over
the yawning cavity at the end, and started the fire.
"This trunk will last as long as we're here," he
said. "When the end burns off we'll just push
it further in. But we'll have to get a good pile of
firewood besides. Our fire's our only protection at
night."

It was getting dark before they sat down for
supper, though the leaping flames gave abundant
illumination. They had buried potatoes in the hot
ashes and they were roasted to a turn. Jimmy had
gone down to the stream, and in fifteen minutes
had caught enough beautiful iridescent trout for
their meal. Evidently in this part of the world,
the wiles of anglers were unknown. A saucepan
filled with tomatoes, emitted an enticing odor, and
there was coffee for those who wanted it. They
ate and drank luxuriously, washed their tin plates
and cups in water heated in an iron kettle, and then
sat around the camp-fire and told stories, till Ruth
went to sleep in her father's arms, and Judy's head
was jerking violently like a poppy blossom in a high
wind. And then, remembering their early start,
Pollyanna declared it bedtime.

A tarpaulin had been thrown over a projecting branch of the big tree to protect the bed in case of rain, but Pollyanna could look out at the sides into a night as black as primeval chaos. Although behind her the fire crackled reassuringly, its heat was little protection against the chill of the night. They had removed only their boots before going to bed. There was one blanket under them, and a whole mound above; but Pollyanna found the warmth of the children's bodies as they cuddled close to her more than welcome. Dorothy moaned once or twice in her sleep, and Pollyanna wondered uneasily if it were due to her being cold, or if it were only the pain of her aching heart. So the pioneer women slept unnumbered times, needing a fire for protection from wild beasts, and perhaps afraid to light it, because of the Indians. To those women, the nights under the stars were not a week's holiday to end in a comfortable home. When the journey ended, it would be in the wilderness, with danger on every hand.

Pollyanna hugged little Ruth tighter. "I'm glad," she murmured drowsily, "*very* glad I live in the twentieth century.

CHAPTER XIX

A NIGHT OF WATCHING

THE first three days were much alike, but nobody minded that. They rose early, for they woke refreshed, and eager to be about the day's activities. Three times a day they caught trout, cleaned trout, cooked trout and ate trout, and they all felt that this program could continue indefinitely. At night they kept up the practice of telling stories around the camp fire, and Arthur's supply, at least, gave no indication of running low. Some of his repertoire was so bizarre, so blood-curdling, indeed, that Pollyanna felt a little anxious on the children's account, till Ruth remarked patronizingly, on one of the occasions when she had remained awake to hear the conclusion of an especially atrocious tale, "Arthur's a funny man, ain't he, Muvver?"

It was the fourth day, and Dorothy had stayed behind when the men went off to fish, to help with the dishes and make partial preparations for the midday meal. About ten o'clock Pollyanna said, "Now, Dorothy, why don't you go fishing? There's nothing else to be done, except put the potatoes to bake, and it's too early for that."

"Why don't you fish today, Mrs. Pendleton, instead of me?"

"There is only one reason, Dorothy, and that is, I don't like fishing. Now sitting here on the pine needles, I'm happy doing nothing. But as soon as I have a fishing rod in my hand, I feel as if I ought to be pulling in a fish every minute."

"You can practically do that here. Of course we put back the small ones."

"Yes, but then there's the fish to be taken off the hook and the worm to be put on." Pollyanna shivered. "There's no arguing about tastes," she quoted. "Go ahead, Dorothy. It's doing you a lot of good up here. You don't know how much better you look."

Dorothy smiled as if the compliment amused, rather than pleased her, and Pollyanna felt uneasy. "You do feel better, don't you, Dorothy?" she coaxed.

"Oh, Mrs. Pendleton, what's the use of talking about it!"

"But I want to know."

"Well, then," the girl said listlessly, "I really can't see the use of going on living. Nothing has savor any more. Everything's spoiled."

"Oh, Dorothy," Pollyanna remonstrated, even while she told herself that the girl was exaggerating. It might be true that everything had lost its savor, but for all that, Dorothy was eating three good meals a day. And she had seemed really triumphant one afternoon when she had brought home a larger trout than either Jimmy or Arthur could boast. As these thoughts fluttered through Pollyanna's mind, Dorothy said with a sigh, "Thank heaven, I don't belong to a long-lived family."

"Don't say such things, Dorothy. Long before your time comes, your life will be as precious to you as mine is to me."

Dorothy answered with an expressive shrug, and taking up her fishing rod, went down the slope toward the river. And Pollyanna, resolving that she would not allow her spirits to be overcast by the dejection she suspected was half a pose, sat with her back against the biggest spruce of all, and gave herself up to absorbing as much as possible of the scene. There was a book or two, brought along as a sort of insurance against rain, but she did not feel in the mood for reading. There were writing materials handy, but she had temporarily lost all interest in her correspondence. She wanted to see everything that was to be seen, to drink in the composite fragrance brought by every breeze, to feel the sun in her eyes, and the wind on her cheeks, and the pine needles under her, to hear above the brook's monotonous babble, the cawing of a crow, and more rarely, the song of a bird, carrying his springtime rapture over into the late summer. Junior and Judy were fishing at the brook in plain sight. Ruth was trotting around, picking up pine cones to burn at the camp-fire. Pollyanna felt that her cup of well-being overflowed.

At half-past eleven, she aroused herself to put the potatoes in the ashes, and open two cans of the perennially popular baked beans. The fishermen would be up by noon. As a rule they cleaned their fish at the brook's edge, flinging the offal back into the stream to nourish the catch for next day.

It was about twelve by her wrist watch, when the men came in sight, though their voices had been audible several minutes before. Pollyanna scrambled to her feet. Now was the time to play the role of energetic housewife.

She waved her hand as the two approached, and soon was indulging in her customary, but by no means pretended ecstasies, over the beauty of the fish. Not till she had her frying pan in place, did she ask, "Where is Dorothy?"

Jimmy looked up surprised. "Dorothy! Why, we haven't seen her."

"You haven't? Why, she went down to join you about ten o'clock."

Arthur chuckled. "Don't you remember, Mr. Pendleton, we told her she talked too much. A woman never likes that, you know. Why doesn't she, Mrs. Pendleton?"

"Perhaps," suggested Pollyanna, a trifle absent-mindedly, "she knows that even if she says a good deal, it is worth hearing."

"I'll call her," Arthur continued. "Guess she won't stand on her dignity enough to skip a meal. Dorothy's not very big, but there's nothing wrong with her appetite."

He put his hands to his lips, and sent the girl's name ringing across the valley. "Dor-o-thy! Dor-o-thy!" And then as the minutes passed, he drew his revolver, and fired several shots into the air. The mountains tossed the echoes back and forth, till the effect was like a salvo of artillery. But Dorothy did not appear.

Arthur came back up the slope, frowning a little. "Oh, well, we'll have grub," he said. "Serves her right if we eat it all, and don't leave her a mouthful."

There was little danger of that, for Pollyanna's appetite quite deserted her, and Jimmy confessed that he was not hungry. But Arthur filled his plate, and passed it to be refilled, and the children followed his example. While Pollyanna washed the dishes, the men went about shouting Dorothy's name, but when they returned, they were looking grave.

"Mrs. Pendleton," Arthur began abruptly, "how did Dorothy act when she left you? She wasn't mad about anything, was she?"

"No, Arthur, she wasn't angry. But she seemed —depressed." With an effort, Pollyanna told of Dorothy's parting words. Arthur's face remained as imperturbable as an Indian's but Pollyanna saw her husband wince.

"Well, girls' talk don't mean much," was Arthur's comment. "But I guess Mr. Pendleton and I had better put in the afternoon looking for her."

"Arthur," Pollyanna began, with a sudden terrifying sense of the vastness of this wilderness. "Wouldn't it be better to go back for help? Twenty men wouldn't be too many. And there are only two of you."

The young man looked at her in surprise. "Why, no, Mrs. Pendleton, that wouldn't do at all. We'd have to go back to our wagon, and that would take us till well into the night. Before we could get together a crowd of men, and be back here, another night would be on us. We've got to use the time right now."

"Are there any settlers in this valley?" Jimmy asked.

"There are two—a woman and her daughter. Old man Judd was a trapper, and I don't know but the women do a little trapping. They're characters— the mother, especially, pretty near six feet, with a voice like a man's. Folks who wonder that two women should stay up here all winter take it all back when they see the two Judds."

"I only thought," explained Jimmy, "that if there were any settlers near, we'd better let them know of Dorothy's disappearance."

"Yes, we'll let them know. Their cabin is across the river, and about five miles down the valley, but we might as well go there as anywhere else. Now let's get our horses. You can take Spot, and I'll ride Sam."

Five minutes later the two men rode out of camp, and as a relief from overwhelming nervousness, Pollyanna fell to work. She collected quantities of firewood, and the children, feeling the contagion of her energy, lent her valuable assistance. They were less enthusiastic when she suggested that it was an ideal time for a bath all round, but they yielded submissively, and behind the sheltering tarpaulin, Pollyanna scrubbed all three, in rapid succession.

While she marked time, the two men had ridden east, and it was not long before they found a clew, Dorothy's fishing rod flung down beside a natural path some ten feet from the river. Arthur looked it over and then handed it to Jimmy.

"It's hers, all right," Jimmy said, examining the rod. "It hasn't been used today."

Arthur swung himself from his horse. "It's clear she didn't want to fish," he said. "I'm going to see if I can find any signs that she went down to the river from here."

He took some minutes for his examination, but came back shaking his head. Then the two followed the windings of the river, calling Dorothy's name, and sometimes firing a shot. When they came opposite the point where the Judd cabin stood, they forded the stream and rode up to the door.

Mrs. Judd was sitting on the doorstep, but she rose, as they approached, and stood with her hand on the gun thrust negligently into her belt. She was a formidable woman, apart from her weapon. Her short calico dress revealed heavy legs, which not inappropriately disappeared in a pair of men's boots. Under her contracted brows, her eyes were suspicious.

Arthur explained his errand which Mrs. Judd seemed to regard as an effort at humor. "You want

to know ef we've seen a gal runnin' 'round these
here mountains? Why, ef we saw a gal, we'd be
plumb shore 'twas a ghost o' somebody. 'Druther
see a grizzly any day."

"Your daughter didn't see her, either, I suppose?"

"I'll ask her." Mrs. Judd opened the door of
the cabin and spoke to someone inside. "Elmira,
there's two men here, who want to know ef you've
seed a gal wanderin' 'round. Short she is, and
short-haired. What d'ye say? Yes, ain't it?"

She shut the door, and looked the two men over,
with what seemed malicious amusement. "Elmira
thinks that's a joke," she said.

"Not to us," Jimmy replied gravely, and rather
ironically, thanked her for her courtesy. The woman
stared at them from under her bushy brows, and
silently watched them take their departure.

Pollyanna had supper ready at six o'clock, except
for the coffee, which would not take long, since the
water was boiling. At quarter of seven, she fed
the children and put sleepy Ruth to bed. As darkness came on she piled wood on the fire, for her
nerves were jumpy. That afternoon something had
happened that had given her an odd feeling at the
pit of her stomach. Pointing to a rocky ledge in
the distance, Judy had exclaimed, "Mother, that
looks like a bear."

Pollyanna glanced in the direction indicated by the slender fore-finger, and smiled her approval of the small girl's cleverness. "It does look rather like a bear, dear," she acknowledged indulgently. "It's really some funny old stump."

Five minutes later, Ruth pulled at her sleeve. "Muvver, that funny old stump's gone walking."

Pollyanna whirled about. The ledge to which Judy had called her attention gleamed grey in the sun. There was no sign of the dark patch which had suggested a ruminating bear. And Pollyanna realized, as if it were an entirely new idea, that she and her children were in the heart of the wilderness, with a hostile life hidden from them by a screen of leaves. Though it was still bright daylight, she went back and built up the fire.

It was dark when the men came in. Pollyanna hastened to make the coffee, asking no questions. And not till they had eaten, did they speak of the matter uppermost in the minds of all.

"Well, we haven't had any luck," Arthur said. "Except that she dropped her fishing rod out here, not an eighth of a mile away. We've yelled and we've fired and there hasn't been any answer. It don't look as if there were much use to hunt to-night, but I'm going to take the rifle, and do my best."

"I'll go with you," Jimmy said.

"No, siree!" Arthur cried. "We brought along two women and three children, and we're responsible for all of them. You stay here and look after your own."

"I—I—can—get along," Pollyanna faltered. Probably she had never said four words that had cost her such an effort.

"Maybe, but you're not going to try," retorted Arthur bluntly. "If something has happened to Dorothy, that's bad enough. But we won't take any chances with the rest of you."

He drank cup after cup of the coffee, made a couple of sandwiches and thrust them into his pocket, then stood up. "See you later," he said jauntily, and picking up his rifle, vanished into the dark. And Pollyanna sat with her face turned from the fire, that the others might not see the tears rolling down her cheeks. The older children were too subdued to ask for the usual stories. Shortly after Arthur's departure, they went to bed, a simple process, since all that was necessary in the way of preparations was to remove their shoes. Jimmy followed them almost immediately. "You're not going to sit up, are you?" he asked Pollyanna. "I'm afraid it's no use."

"Oh, no, I'm going to bed. Put on plenty of

wood, Jimmy," she added nervously. "We can get another big pile tomorrow."

But in bed she found it impossible to sleep. She wondered if she had said the wrong thing to Dorothy, and what the right thing would have been. The conviction was growing on her, and on Jimmy, too, she was sure, that Dorothy had taken her own life. Blameless as she knew herself to be, it was inevitable that Pollyanna should reproach herself for not knowing intuitively the girl's desperate mood.

When lying quiet became intolerable, she left her bed and sat by the blazing fire. The sound of the rushing water and the crackle of flames gave her an odd feeling of companionship. These two friends of man, water and fire, were hers to command here in the wilderness. She could not feel altogether lonely, with the voice of the water in her ears and the warmth of the fire on her face.

The tarpaulin hanging over the other bed, swayed, and Jimmy came toward her. He sat down beside her, and took her hand. "Can't you sleep, dear?"

"No, but I wish you could, Jimmy. You must be terribly tired."

"I'm tired, but I can't sleep. That poor girl! I'm afraid she's drowned herself, Pollyanna. It's hardly possible that she would stray away into the wilderness unless she was quite out of her mind."

"Oh, Jimmy, if only I—"

"Hush, darling. You did the best you knew. You never failed in kindness and thoughtfulness. Why, we're up here on her account."

"And I brought her to her death," Pollyanna sobbed.

"Pollyanna, it isn't our fault that God didn't give us the ability to see into the future. If we do our best with the minds He gave us, that's all He has a right to ask of us, and all we should ask of ourselves."

He put his arm around his wife, and drew her to him. Pollyanna's head dropped to his shoulder. For a time she sobbed softly and then, comforted by that strong clasp, she fell asleep. And Jimmy, holding her protectingly, found his own head nodding, and presently he, too, was sleeping.

Arthur came rather early next morning, his face haggard, his eyes ringed with the black circles of desperate fatigue. He ate his breakfast and said to Jimmy, "Now I'm going to lie down and take forty winks."

"Sleep as long as you can, old man. I'll go out this morning."

"You'd better catch a few fish, till I'm ready to start. I'm not going to sleep more than an hour, but I've got to have that. It's seven now. Wake me sure at eight o'clock."

He flung himself on the bed, and was instantly asleep. Pollyanna sent the children off to play at a little distance, and let her work wait. It was unlikely that the clinking of the dishes in her pan would disturb Arthur, but she would take no chances. Jimmy went down to the river, taking Junioı with him. He was back at eight o'clock, and between them they woke Arthur, or partially woke him.

"I can't get it into my head what you want," he said irritably. "Wait a minute!" He staggered down to the brook, dipped his head several times into the icy water, rose with a shake, and was ready for the start.

"Today, Mr. Pendleton," he said, as the two rode out of the camp, "we'll keep an eye on the river. It looks to me as if she'd drowned herself."

"That's what I think too, Arthur. Poor, foolish girl!"

"We'll follow it as far as we can," Arthur said. "When the water's so cold, a body is slow to rise. We'll just have to keep our eyes open for anything a little out of the ordinary."

They were riding on the side of the mountain, several miles from the camp, when Jimmy, as he had done a number of times before, drew his field glasses from their case, and took a sweeping survey of the opposite bank. Suddenly the lines of his figure grew tense, and he leveled the glass at a point some distance down the stream.

"Arthur," he said, his voice sharpened by unmistakable excitement, "What's that clearing down there?"

Arthur's eyes followed the direction of his extended hand. "Why, that's Judd's cabin, where we were yesterday."

"Is the Judd girl a cripple?"

"A cripple? Well, neither you nor I would think so, if we stood up to her in a fair fight. Why?"

"Look and see for yourself."

Arthur focused the glasses on the clearing on the opposite bank, the log house showing distinctly against the green. And with the aid of the glasses, Arthur saw a figure moving across the face of the buildings. It was grotesquely arrayed, the dress touching the ground, and hanging loosely at the shoulders. It was impossible to make out the face. Apparently it was bandaged.

But it was the motion of this extraordinary figure that gripped Arthur's attention. It advanced with singular slowness, wriggling ahead with a queer swaying motion, and then all at once, it made a curious leap, like a bird.

The door opened and a big woman appeared. In one stride she reached the figure with the bandaged face, picked it up as if it had been an infant, and carried it into the house. As Arthur returned the glass, Jimmy saw his hand was shaking.

"I don't know what that means," Arthur said hoarsely, "but it looks like devil's work to me. Anyway, we'll soon find out."

They crossed the river at once, rode for a short distance toward the cabin, and then left their horses and proceeded on foot. There were many outjutting rocks on this side of the river, and they stole from one to the other, till they were close to the cabin. Luck was with them! The formidable Mrs. Judd was at work in her garden, her back toward them.

"I'll attend to her," Arthur whispered. "You wait till I call you, and then run out."

His leap, when he left the rock, made Jimmy think of a puma. He was at the woman's back before she had time to turn. "Up with your hands, Auntie," he shouted. "There's a gun at the back of your neck." As her hands lifted automatically, he reached around her, and took from her belt the gun they had noticed the day before.

"Hi, there, Jim," he yelled, forgetting to give Jimmy his full title. "Come on. It's all right."

Jimmy appeared, wearing a shame-faced expression, as for the first time, he realized that Arthur had laid his plans so as to take all the danger on himself. The woman the forester had disarmed was grinding her teeth, looking in her silent fury rather less than human.

"You go on into the cabin," Arthur directed Jimmy, "And find who that girl is we saw hopping like a toad this morning."

"No, no," cried Mrs. Judd. "No, no!" And then, as Arthur pressed the muzzle of his revolver against her back, she seemed to collapse. The big figure suddenly went limp, swayed as if about to fall.

Jimmy had his own gun in his hand, as he pushed open the cabin door. The daughter of the house, he recalled, was like the mother. But there was only one room in the cabin, and only one occupant of the room, a girl who sat straight and motionless in a chair.

It took Jimmy a moment to realize that the reason she did not stir was that she was strapped into the chair. He looked at her face. It was covered with strips of heavy white cloth, but the eyes above the criss-cross bandages were Dorothy's.

Jimmy uttered a cry and his gun clattered to the floor, as he fumbled for his pocket knife. He slit the disfiguring bandages, and then pulled a wad of similar material from between Dorothy's teeth. "Are you hurt?" he demanded.

"No-o. I guess not," the girl half sobbed. "My feet and arms are tied."

He slashed the rope binding her feet, and that confining her arms, unbuckled the strap, and helped her to rise. "Can't you stand?" he asked dismayed as she swayed and clung to him.

"In a minute. My feet were tied so tight it stopped the circulation."

Jimmy looked her over. "Do you know where your own clothes are? If you do, get them, and I'll step outside while you change." Then he remembered the formidable Miss Judd. "Any danger of the daughter's coming back soon?"

Dorothy shook her head. "She's dead," she whispered, and began limping toward a chest in the corner. After a moment, she drew out her own khaki costume with its divided skirt.

"All right," Jimmy said, and left her to make the welcome change. On the steps he shouted to Arthur, "Dorothy's here and she'll be out in a minute. Her feet were tied and her arms tied behind her back. That's why she hopped when we watched her through the glass."

"Tied her up, did you?" Arthur shook his fist at his captive's sagging back. "What ought a fellow

to do with such an old rattlesnake?" he asked
Jimmy.

He was still relieving his anger by the use of violent and rather picturesque language, when Dorothy
appeared and she checked him. "Oh, don't, Arthur.
She's really not right here," she ended, touching her
forehead.

"She seemed pretty shrewd the other day when
we saw her," Arthur said sulkily. "However, if you
want me to let up on her, I guess I can. But we'll
take her guns along. Look through the house, Mr.
Pendleton, and make a clean sweep. She's a dead
shot, you know."

Over the firearms Jimmy had collected, Arthur
addressed his prisoner. "We're going to take these
with us, but tomorrow, after sun-up, you'll find them
on the trail this side the river, in plain sight. Don't
come looking for 'em any earlier, for if you do,
I'll tie you up the way you tied Miss Blythe here, and
take you to the nearest jail."

The woman had listened stoically to Arthur's various uncomplimentary remarks, but when she saw
Dorothy departing, she broke into a grieved whim-
per. As Dorothy limped along the trail to the waiting horses, she explained.

"You see the poor soul's daughter died last winter—"

"Elmira Judd dead!" exclaimed Arthur. "Why, I thought she spoke to her when we came here yesterday afternoon."

"It was I, sitting there gagged and bound, so I couldn't speak or move. And I heard her tell you I said it was a joke. But all the same, her daughter did die last winter. It was too cold to bury her body, and she kept it frozen in the lean-to to her cabin, and had to watch out for the wolves that came sniffing around. It was no wonder her mind went. And when she saw me—was it only yesterday?—she thought I was her daughter come back."

Arthur relieved his taut nerves by a yell of laughter. "If you'd ever seen Elmira Judd, Dorothy, you'd appreciate the compliment."

But Dorothy had not reached the point where she could see the humor of the situation. "For all I was so terrified, I couldn't help being sorry for her. She didn't tie me at first, but when she saw I meant to get away if I could, she found a rope and tied my feet and hands. She said that after you left the valley, she'd take the ropes off."

They reached the waiting horses at last, and Jimmy put Dorothy on his horse, while he walked at its head. When they came to ford the river, he was ready to walk through it, waist-deep as it was, but Arthur, after addressing him in terms almost as uncomplimentary as he had used to Mrs. Judd, took Dorothy across, helped her dismount, and then brought Jimmy the horse she had been riding. And so about three hours after the men had started out, they came back to camp.

Pollyanna had been struggling to expect Dorothy's return, and had made a dismal failure. When the girl rode into camp, pale and wan, but smiling, Pollyanna for the first time in her life had a touch of hysterics. She laughed till her chest and side pained her excruciatingly, while all the time the tears were streaming down her cheeks. It was a shrewd suggestion of Jimmy's that Dorothy might be hungry that saved the day. Pollyanna rushed to prepare dinner, and while she did an incredible number of foolish things, the customary routine steadied her nerves, and helped her through the crisis. As soon as the meal was ready, she was able to eat with the others.

When there was nothing more to eat, she looked across at Arthur. "Is it too late to start for home this afternoon?" she asked.

"This afternoon! Why, you've got two days more."

"I know," Pollyanna swallowed, "but somehow I feel as if I'd had enough."

"I don't think we should start before morning,"

Jimmy objected. "You know Arthur didn't get any sleep last night, and you and I weren't much better."

"I didn't sleep," Dorothy admitted, "but all the same I'd like to start for home."

"I don't know but I feel that way myself," said Arthur unexpectedly. "You see we tried to bring along the Judd arsenal, but nobody knows where the old woman has a six-shooter tucked away. I'd feel better if we were out of this valley."

With that statement of opinion, they fell to work. The luxurious camp beds were abandoned, the blankets rolled up, the remaining provisions stuffed into sacks and loaded on the burros. "You've got the better of me, Mrs. Pendleton," Arthur said. "We've got food to carry home, but if we'd stayed two days longer, there'd have been mighty little." And Pollyanna admitted that he was right.

Early in the afternoon, they said good-by to the brook and the guardian trees, and started homeward. A short time before, Jimmy had crossed the river and deposited Mrs. Judd's "arsenal," as Arthur called it, on the trail they had followed earlier in the day. They were all disposed to talk a good deal, and to laugh when there was nothing especial to laugh about, and when Pollyanna and Dorothy caught each other's eyes, they smiled broadly, as if they shared some very amusing secret.

As they took the sharp pitch that was the beginning of the mountain trail, Pollyanna looked back over her shoulder. The valley they were leaving was as beautiful as she had thought it at first, but Pollyanna sincerely hoped she would never see it again.

CHAPTER XX

Dearest Aunt Ruth:

It is quite early in the morning, much earlier than I usually sit down to write letters, but that "little spark of celestial fire" as somebody called the conscience, has been approaching the proportions of a conflagration the last few days, whenever, in fact, I have thought of you. Can it be possible that I have written you only once since Christmas, and that an acknowledgment of your wonderful Christmas box? It doesn't seem possible, yet I'm afraid it's so.

Probably you think, just as I thought, when I looked forward to this winter, that time would hang heavily on my hands. But instead I've been busier than ever, and such a nice, happy sort of "busyness," too. Out here a radio set is a social magnet, especially in the winter, when everybody has less to do. I wish you could see my living-room filled with people on a stormy night, listening to Walter Damrosch's musicians and to his explanations of the music. I think he is the prime favorite with our audience, though the Jubilee singers rank very high.

260

The library is going stronger than ever, and I want to thank you for the last box of books which were sorely needed to take the place of a number of volumes that had literally been read to pieces. I am hoping before the winter is over to make readers out of almost every ranch woman in this valley. The lives of some of them are a dead grind through the twelve months of the year, and apparently the idea of enjoying themselves, never enters their heads. A few, of course, are too ignorant to get any pleasure out of books, but the majority can learn to like reading. And many—thanks to the books you send—are already finding life thrilling far beyond their modest expectations.

I hope I don't bore you writing so much about Luke Geist, but when I remember the young man I first visited nine months ago, and how ready he seemed to curse God and die, I don't feel at all that the day of miracles is over. Mattie Murray deserves as much credit as I, for it was she who started him on the Glad Game and he plays it in a way that makes me ashamed. But I flatter myself it was something I said that inspired him to find out what he could do with his brains. Mattie helps him as best she can, and is very much embarrassed when he calls her his "teacher." As a matter of fact, he is much quicker than she, though she has had more schooling, and he helps her as much as she helps him. I could see a nice little romance budding there if the poor boy wasn't such an invalid. But people sometimes recover after such accidents, I am sure.

You see I am trying to make this letter lead up to a climax, the way we learned in school. I've begun with the people you don't know, and now I've come to the ones you do know and love. The children are simply wonderful. I'm glad Jimmy isn't here to read this over my shoulder and smile, in that superior way of his, though as a matter of fact he's just as proud of them as I am. Junior is growing so manly, and Judy is a dear, and little Ruth, your namesake, is adorable. She shocked her brother and sister terribly the other day, when she tried to tell the story of Peter's walking on the water, and called him "Peter Rabbit." Junior and Judy immediately undertook to enlighten her, but I'm not sure that she realizes even now the difference between the great apostle and her favorite character in fiction.

Ruth has been insisting lately on "going to school" in the morning, along with the others. Dorothy says she will be reading before we know it, but as long as we don't push her a bit, just tell her what she insists on knowing, I can't see that it will do any harm. Wasn't Macaulay quite a Greek scholar when he was five or so? Of course Ruth isn't a Macaulay,

and I'm glad she isn't, for it would be very embarrassing to have one of your children using the long
words he was so fond of, and which you'd have to
look up in the dictionary before you could make a
suitable reply.

And the children have been so well, Aunt Ruth.
Of course we don't take any chances. As soon as
one of them seems a little ailing, we take his temperature—or hers, as the case may be—and if there is
the least bit of fever, the patient is packed off to bed.
We have had the doctor only once, and that was for
Nancy, who took a bad cold late in January. He
seemed a very trustworthy man, and he ought to be,
for in addition to his duties as a general practitioner,
he performs operations for appendicitis, and ampu
tates limbs, all in the day's work.

To show what a doctor has to contend with in
this part of the world, he told me of one of his
patients who, after giving birth to a new baby, was
very ill. The oldest child, a little girl of nine, acted
as nurse and housekeeper. When the doctor got
there one morning, the little girl had just prepared
the baby's bottle. It was filled with strong tea, and
was so hot that she had wrapped it in a towel in order
to be able to handle it. That, of course, was an
extreme case, even for this section, but the stories
one hears makes one wonder how any of the babies

live to grow up. Yet, judging by appearances, there is no danger of race suicide in this part of the world.

Dorothy is more of a joy every day. Just before that dreadful experience in the mountains, of which I wrote you last fall, she was terribly depressed. You know how young people sometimes feel when things go wrong, as if life wasn't worth living? But those hours in the Judd cabin opened her eyes, and I believe that now she's grateful for every new day of life. The two young men who are constantly coming here, Clifford and Arthur, are both devoted to her. They are splendid fellows, both of them, and I hope some day she will like one of them well enough to marry him, but which is the favorite only Dorothy herself knows, if indeed, *she* does.

Jimmy is working hard and developing splendidly. I can just see him grow—mentally I mean—though he is filling out physically, and getting to be quite a magnificent specimen.

Have I ever told you that our Pluto left us? Apparently the call of the wild was too much for him, but I'm in hopes that with the return of spring, we shall hear his familiar caw again, and that he will light on my shoulder some fine morning, and drop something down my neck. Puck has gone through the winter finely, and is really an imposing animal now, with his funny little horns. Jiggs and he continue their queer friendship. I often wonder what they say, when they talk us over.

Dearest Aunt Ruth, doesn't this long letter atone for my neglect? Do prove you forgive me by writing very soon to

Your penitent and loving
Pollyanna.

CHAPTER XXI

JIGGS TURNS HERO

IT really was a wonderful day. Jiggs felt so good himself that he was not surprised by the singular actions of his friend, Puck. When interrupted in cropping the grass by Jiggs' approach to the enclosure, Puck lowered his head, and came at him with a rush. Then unable to reach Jiggs, with his short, sharp horns, he stood pawing the ground with his forefoot, in a highly irascible fashion. But Jiggs only wagged his tail. He knew how to take a joke.

Jiggs was aware that he was to have a busy day. At the breakfast table, his Mistress had said something about house cleaning, and his Master had protested. "Oh, you women!" the Master had said. "Why can't you enjoy the spring, without turning the house bottom-side up?"

The Master was a good master, none better, but the Mistress was always right. She gave her reasons for cleaning house. Jiggs did not pay much attention since he knew, without listening, that they were unanswerable. He merely told himself that if the house was to be turned upside down, he must be on hand to help.

When after this little encounter with Puck, he went to find his Mistress, she was in an upstairs bedroom and the rugs had been rolled into a bundle, and the mattresses were on the floor. Jiggs pressed close to Pollyanna's ankles, and Pollyanna stooped and patted him. "Come to help me, have you Jiggs?" Trust his Mistress to understand.

Nancy was not at all like the Mistress. When she came upstairs, she looked askance at the small dog. "If ever there was an animal who liked to make a nuisance of hisself, it's that there Jiggs," said Nancy. "Now why can't he go and lie under the trees, same as he would if we wasn't so busy?"

"He wants to help, Nancy," the Mistress laughed. "Wait! We'll throw those rugs out of the window and leave them for the Schroeder boy. He promised to be here by ten."

If Jiggs had not known the Mistress was always right, he would have been inclined to suspect that on this particular occasion, the Master had spoken words of wisdom. For they did queer things, those two women. It made him uncomfortable to have all the familiar furniture in the wrong places, and the bed stripped to its bones—he supposed those queer, wiry things under the mattress were its bones. And

the smell of soap suds, which reminded him un-
pleasantly of taking a bath, was so strong that it
drowned out the delicious odor of beef stewing
slowly on the kitchen stove. Had Jiggs not been so
determined to stand by his Mistress when she needed
him, he would have fled from the house, till that
upheaval known as house-cleaning was over.

At twelve o'clock they stopped for luncheon,
which, in Jiggs' opinion, was the most sensible
thing they had done since morning. And then Dorothy suggested taking the children for a walk. "With
all these flowers springing up everywhere, they'll
simply imbibe botany; they just can't help it."

The Mistress approved the idea. "You might take
Jiggs with you," she suggested.

"Yes'm, I hope so," said Nancy from the kitchen.
"Soon as you get a piece of floor washed up, that
dog has to walk across it, and then walk back again,
sniffing all the time. I don't say he's a bad dog, as
dogs go, but at house-cleaning time, a nuisance is a
nuisance."

Jiggs listened with dignity. When Dorothy and
the children were ready to start, they called him, and
Jiggs walked over and seated himself at his Mistress' feet. They all understood that he preferred to
stay with her, but no one realized that his refusal to
go walking represented supreme fidelity to duty.

With Jiggs' assistance, Pollyanna was making gratifying progress in getting the upstairs rooms to rights, when Nancy, who had remained in the kitchen to attend to some dinner preparations, came hurrying up the stairs. "Miss Pollyanna," she exclaimed in a voice of consternation. "That young man's here again."

"What young man?"

"Well, I s'pose he's got two good Christian names, such as other folks, but the only one I've ever heerd anybody use is Jerry."

"Jerry!" Pollyanna repeated, amazed. "You don't mean that Jerry has had the audacity to come to this house?"

"He had the 'dasity to ride up to our door and jump off his horse. I guess that'll be him now." For at that moment, a loud rapping was distinctly audible on the second floor.

"I'll see him," said Pollyanna grimly. She took off her dusting cap and apron, and kneeling before the mirror, which was leaning against the wall, instead of hanging in its accustomed place, she hastily smoothed her hair. Had she been in a mood to notice such things, she would have seen that the mirror gave back an attractive reflection. Pollyanna's cheeks had flamed up when Nancy announced her caller. Her eyes were flashing. Jiggs put his head on one side and gazed at her wonderingly. Nancy thought, "They don't make 'em better looking than that girl."

When Pollyanna got downstairs, Jerry was sitting on one of the rocking-chairs on the porch. "Didn't know whether you were going to let me in," he drawled. "Thought I might as well be comfortable, while you were making up your mind." He added with an ingratiating smile, "Dorothy anywhere around, Mrs. Pendleton?"

"No, she isn't," Pollyanna replied. "And if she were, I don't know why she should care to see you."

"Oh, come, Mrs. Pendleton," Jerry coaxed. "Things aren't as bad as all that."

"Not as bad—" Pollyanna realized she was speaking too loudly, checked herself and finished in a lower tone, "You don't seem to realize you've acted outrageously."

"Now listen, Mrs. Pendleton. I'm not going to say I did right, but I want to explain to you just what happened. It's God's truth that I liked Dorothy better than any girl I ever knew. And I was tickled to death when I found she liked me."

Had Pollyanna been older, the rush of blood to her head might have proved fatal. As it was, she answered in a strangled voice, "Her friends couldn't believe that she could care for you—that way."

"Well, it was possible all right," Jerry laughed light-heartedly. "And the last time I talked to her—the last time she came to see me at the hospital—I honestly thought we were going to be happy ever after. And then that little cuss of an Angie had to go ahead and spill the beans."

"Listen to me a moment," Pollyanna interrupted icily. "If you think you're making things any better by throwing the blame on a woman—"

"Old man Adam did that very thing, didn't he, and I've got some of his blood in my veins, I reckon. But whether it's a nice thing to say or not, Mrs. Pendleton, it's true. She came purring around me like a pussy cat, till I didn't know whether I was on my head or my heels."

"It shows how undeserving you were of a fine girl like Dorothy, if right away, you'd let another woman wind you around her finger."

"I'm not saying I did right, but I do say I'm no worse than most fellows, married men and all. That little cuss had me going. It was like coming down with something, and having a high fever, and coming to after a while, and wondering what the devil you'd been doing. It wasn't three weeks till I was sick of that girl, and would have given anything to make Dorothy forget."

"She never will forget," Pollyanna declared emphatically. "And you haven't any right to ask it of her. You never were her equal in anything. Now you've proved that you're not even a man."

"Oh, I say, Mrs. Pendleton!" Jerry's face reddened with the vehemence of his remonstrance.

"Dorothy isn't the only girl you've treated unfairly. Look at Minnie Walker. You threw her over when Dorothy came, just as you dropped Dorothy for that nurse."

In spite of his penitence, Jerry could not control the flicker of a complacent smirk, and this added fuel to the fires of Pollyanna's wrath. She went on hurriedly, "Oh, I know, Jerry, this is all food to your vanity. It makes you feel how irresistible you are, when a nice girl is miserable for months because you made love to her and then threw her away like a plaything you were tired of."

"Poor old Min," Jerry said, not unkindly, and then added persuasively, "but after all, Mrs. Pendleton, you can't expect a fellow to take Minnie, when he can get Dorothy."

Pollyanna was breathing hard. "Well, your folly and weakness have settled that. You can't get Dorothy now."

"That remains to be seen," Jerry drawled, and she knew he was angry at last. "That's for Dorothy to say. Nobody can speak for her."

"I won't have her troubled," Pollyanna was beginning, and then she stopped short, with a feeling
of utter helplessness, for at that moment she heard
Dorothy's voice in the kitchen. She remembered the
influence this picturesque cowboy had had over the
girl from the first. Dorothy's face, as it had looked
when she told her she meant to marry Jerry, came
vividly before her. Now that he had come back penitent, how would she receive him?

Jerry, too, had heard Dorothy's voice, as was evident from the brightening of his face. "Why,
there's the little girl herself," he cried, and rose to
his feet as if to go in search of her.

As it proved, this was unnecessary. Dorothy must
have heard his ringing voice, or perhaps she had
noticed his horse outside. She appeared almost
immediately in the door of the living-room. The
young man made a quick step toward her, and seized
her hands.

"Dorothy!" he cried, "if you're not a sight for
sore eyes! Look here, little girl, I know I ought to
start in saying I'm sorry, and all that sort of thing,
but all I can think of is that I'm doggoned glad to
see you."

"And I'm glad to see you, Jerry," Dorothy said
quietly, making no effort to withdraw her hands
from his. "I hoped you'd come."

Pollyanna actually groaned aloud. There was no hope, she saw, of saving a girl, determined to make shipwreck of her life. She rose to her feet, feeling that she must get away from the harrowing spectacle of Jerry holding Dorothy's hands, and beaming down upon her with an air of proud possession. But Dorothy heard her movement and turned quickly. "Please don't go, Mrs. Pendleton," she said.

"No, don't go, Mrs. Pendleton," Jerry echoed. "She wouldn't believe that you'd forgive me, girlie. I want her to stay till she's found out you do."

"Of course, I forgive you, Jerry," said the girl. "The one I blame is myself, my stupidity and ignorance and vanity. You couldn't have hurt and humiliated me as you did, if I hadn't put the weapons in your hands."

Jerry looked uncomfortable. "Let's not talk about it, sweetie," he begged. "I've been kicking myself for the last three months. That little cuss, Angie—"

"No, we won't talk about it," Dorothy interrupted. "It was my fault. The fact is, I'd never seen anyone like you before. You are good-looking, you know, and you're a picturesque figure. You represented Romance to me. I was silly enough to think that the men you can always count on, the loyal, reliable men, who'd rather die than hurt the woman they love, were sort of commonplace. 'Standard-ized,' I called them. Wasn't I a fool?"

Pollyanna, who had been standing since her im-pulse to flight had been checked, slumped into a chair. She was trembling with excitement, waiting breathlessly for what was coming next. She saw that Jerry's face had lost its smiling complacency, that he looked worried.

"But that was a long time ago," Dorothy went on. "It's a long time since that dance at Deer Creek, isn't it? Of course, I forgive you, Jerry, for no-body but you could have taught me what you did that night. It wasn't an easy lesson, but it's the kind you learn once and never forget."

"Look here, Dorothy   "

"Wait, Jerry. I'm glad you came today, for I want to tell you that I'm going to marry Clifford. Of course he's too good for me. I couldn't be worthy of him in a thousand years, but I believe I can make him happy. At least I'm going to try. And I'm sure you wish us joy."

He dropped her hands and took a backward step. "You're going to marry—old Cliff?"

"Yes."

His face twitched. "Well, I guess I deserve it."

"That's more than is true of either of us," Doro-thy replied. "Clifford deserves something better, and I don't deserve anything at all. But that doesn't matter, since we're both satisfied."

Pollyanna could endure it no longer. She opened her arms and Dorothy flung herself into them, and cried on her shoulder. It seemed to Jerry a good time to withdraw, and picking up his hat, he left the room without a word. But it was only a moment before the raptures of the two women were interrupted by screams.

When Dorothy brought her charges back from their walk, she had recognized Jerry's horse standing in the front yard. "You'd better stay outside and play awhile," she told the children, and entering by the kitchen door, said a word to Nancy, by way of announcing herself, and walked through to the living-room. Hardly had she entered the house, when Minnie Walker rode into the yard, a package of books from Pollyanna's library tied to her saddle.

Since the dance at Deer Creek, Minnie had seemed a different girl. If there is truth in the saying that misery loves company, that may have accounted for the marked improvement in her spirits. Since Dorothy was a fellow-sufferer, rather than a successful rival, hostility was uncalled-for. She had begun to draw books from Pollyanna's library, and had attended a number of the radio evenings.

But whatever serenity Minnie had attained by the discovery that Jerry was capable of jilting other girls as well as herself, it was threatened when she saw his horse standing at the Pendletons' porch. She alighted and went a few steps toward the house, then stopped short and beckoned to Junior. The small boy came at once, surprised, and also impressed by her air of mystery.

"Listen!" She clutched his arm, and her hand felt hot through the sleeve of his blouse. "Whose horse is that?"

Junior looked in the direction she indicated. "I don't know."

"It's Jerry's, isn't it?"

"Maybe. It looks kind of like his horse. But he hasn't been here for a long time."

"Oh, he hasn't." Minnie's grip of Junior's arm relaxed. "When was he here last?"

"Oh, I can't remember. But I guess it was before he got hurt. And that was last summer, wasn't it?"

"Yes, last summer." Minnie's face showed profound relief. "But that's his horse now, sure as God made little apples."

"If you want to see him," Junior suggested, "come on in."

Minnie Walker spurned the suggestion. "No," she said. "I'll wait." The new animation of her face was eclipsed by the old sullenness, as she stood waiting for Jerry to appear.

While Junior made himself entertaining to the caller, and Judy played on the porch, little Ruth had dropped down on the back steps, her face as pink as her frock after a long walk. And for some mysterious reason, Puck found the spectacle disquieting. He stamped his feet angrily, tossing his head with its new ornamental appendages. Jiggs, who had come downstairs when his aid was no longer needed in house cleaning, looked indulgently at his queer friend. Evidently Puck was still in a playful mood.

Even as he watched him, a strange thing happened. For the first time Puck jumped the fence surrounding the enclosure, and with lowered head, came straight for Ruth. The deer had been friendly with all the children, and hitherto it would not have occurred to Ruth to be afraid of him. But at the sight of that lowered head, some dormant instinct awoke in the child. She screamed shrilly, and climbed to her feet, fumbling at the latch of the kitchen door.

Before the deer could reach her, Jiggs had launched himself between the two. Growling, snapping, leaping now toward his friend's throat, and now nipping his legs, he diverted the deer's unreasoning rage from Ruth to himself. When Jerry opened the door, a terrified child scrambled past him, and he saw Puck, his head ominously lowered, driving Jiggs toward the side of the barn.

For all Puck's youth, Jiggs was no match for him. Could he have caught the deer by the throat, he would doubtless have held fast, with a grip worthy of his bull-dog ancestors, but though he leaped for the throat, he fell far short of the mark. Puck was quick, and Jiggs was slow, and when the little dog backed, snarling, against the barn, the two dagger-like growths, which had seemed to work such a change in Puck's disposition, menaced him relentlessly.

Junior began to scream. "He's going to kill Jiggs. Puck's going to kill Jiggs. Oh! Oh!"

Jerry clapped his hand to his belt. Had he brought a gun he would have shot the deer instantly, but that morning, his thoughts had been on wooing rather than sterner things. But one of Nancy's clothes poles leaned against the house, and seizing this, he rushed to Jiggs' rescue.

Had he delayed a minute, he would have been too late to save Jiggs' life. For the awkward little dog, out of breath from his jumping, fell over on the side, and his vitals were menaced by those sharp new horns. But Jerry running to the rescue, yelled a warning that Puck heeded.

Behind the audacity of adolescence was the

timidity of the deer tribe. Capable fighters when put to it, the race to which Puck belonged had trusted to their heels rather than their horns, except when the sex instinct had the upper hand. Jerry's rush and the accompanying shout were too much for the mock courage which briefly had transformed the gentle deer. He leaped to one side and was away like a flash of light. And Jiggs, wasting no time, began to lick his torn belly, grunting from pain and excitement. His muzzle was smeared with blood, Puck's and his own, and his loyal dog-heart was hammering furiously against his ribs.

The scream which plucked Pollyanna and Dorothy out of each other's arms had a triple source. Ruth was screaming in the kitchen, Junior was screaming over the danger threatening Jiggs, and Minnie Walker was screaming as danger threatened Jerry. As the young man threw down the pole, that he had had no chance to use, Minnie ran up to him. "Are you hurt, Jerry? Oh, are you hurt?"

Even Jiggs raised his head to glare at her. Her inquiry was clearly preposterous. Since Puck had fled at Jerry's coming, there was no possible chance for him to be hurt. Absurd as her anxiety was from Jiggs' point of view, the accent of tender concern fell sweetly on Jerry's ears. He looked the girl in the eye.

"Well, what if I *was* hurt? Guess you wouldn't care."

"Oh, Jerry." She burst into uncontrollable sobs, and covered her face with her hands.

The young fellow watched her silently. Some of Pollyanna's comments on his conduct had hurt more than he was likely to admit, and Dorothy's frankness had been a bitter, unaccustomed draught. But here was a girl who loved him whatever he did, who loved him when he made her the laughing-stock of the valley; a girl he could pick up when he chose, and throw away when he was ready, without changing her feeling toward him. It was on this model, Jerry told himself, that the Lord should have made all women.

He put his arm through hers, noting that she quivered at the touch, "You don't want anything here, do you, Min?"

"No, no!"

"You're horseback, I see. We'll ride along together."

They were walking arm in arm toward Minnie's horse, when Pollyanna came out on the doorstep. She had stopped in the kitchen to soothe Ruth's incomprehensible terror, and now Junior met her with a story she could hardly have believed, if it were not for the fact that Puck had disappeared and that

Jiggs was hurt. She stooped over the little dog, her heart beating wildly. If Junior was right, Jiggs had saved the baby from injuries at least as serious as his own. And Jerry had saved Jiggs. She wanted to call him back and thank him, perhaps suggest that bygones be bygones. But Jerry helped Minnie to her horse, leaped into his own saddle, and rode away beside the girl without looking back.

CHAPTER XXII

FRIENDS FROM AFAR

IT was such a disagreeable noise! Pollyanna turned on her pillow and shook her head impatiently, as if to shake the sound out of her ears. These tactics proving unsuccessful, she drowsily opened her eyes. Who was hammering, and why?

It was not hammering that she heard. Somebody was knocking. The realization jerked her upright, and cleared the fog from her brain. She was alone in the house, she remembered, for when Dorothy had suggested driving to Deer Creek, she had made some imperative letters an excuse for declining, and suggested that she take Nancy and the children. And then by way of catching up with her correspondence, she had thrown herself on the bed and fallen to sleep instantly. She had no way of knowing how long that knocking had continued, but it seemed to her the sound had been hammering against her ear-drums for hours and hours.

Without even waiting for that glance in the mirror which her sex regards as the essential prelude to most things in life, from interviewing the ice-man to marriage, Pollyanna shot down the stairs, and rushed to open the door. She had a mental picture of some ranchwoman, who had come for a book, standing on the steps, and knocking with the steady persistence that characterized all her activities. When she opened the door on a smiling gentleman, whose overcoat sufficiently differentiated him from the residents of the valley, Pollyanna stared at him blankly, nothing in her expression indicating that she had ever seen him before. Then she finished waking up, and with a shriek of ecstasy threw her arms about his neck.

"Uncle John! Oh, dear, darling Uncle John! Please tell me I'm not dreaming."

"Pollyanna!" cried a voice from the car that stood before the house, "If you don't stop hugging and kissing that man, and pay some attention to me, I warn you I'm going to be jealous."

"Aunt Ruth!" Pollyanna shrieked, and without waiting for Mrs. Pendleton to leave the car, she rushed precipitately into her arms. It was a full minute before she became aware that a second man was sitting beside Aunt Ruth, apparently enjoying the spectacle she was making of herself. She suddenly straightened up, and looked at him, wild-eyed.

"My dear young lady," said the man, who wore eye-glasses and a short, pointed beard, "I have always heard a great deal about Western hospitality, but I had never dreamed it would take so delightful a form. I can only hope that in this particular instance, it has not exhausted itself before getting around to me."

"This is our friend and neighbor, Dr. Davies," said Mrs. Pendleton, laughing at Pollyanna's blank expression. "He is going on with us to California."

Pollyanna had recovered herself. "I really don't know what might have happened, if you had come first," she said, extending her hand. "Providing I had known you were from Boston. But by now, I'm afraid my Western exuberance is running low."

"On our return trip," replied the doctor gallantly, "I shall insist on being the one to knock."

Pollyanna had now discovered another acquaintance, the uniformed chauffeur, who had sat as straight and rigid as a tailor's dummy, till she recognized him. "Why, it's Mark," Pollyanna cried delightedly, putting out her hand to him. "How are you, Mark?"

"I hope I see you well, Mrs. Pendleton," said Mark, touching his cap, and regarding her hand with some embarrassment. However, as Pollyanna showed no intention of taking it away, he shook it modestly and said, "Thank you, ma'am." His manners were so good, his voice so nicely modulated, that

Pollyanna realized if they had met him in the valley, they would have regarded him as a social asset. It really seemed a pity that he should be so embarrassed over shaking hands, and that Aunt Ruth should look as if she didn't quite like it.

Pollyanna jumped lightly from the car. "Why are we all sitting here?" she demanded peremptorily. "Why doesn't everybody get out and come in?"

"Well, you see, dear," Mrs. Pendleton explained, "Since we've taken you by surprise, and since there are several of us, we thought we'd have you direct us to some hotel or inn. It doesn't matter if it is very primitive."

"Here it is!" Pollyanna waved her hand in the direction of her home. "Pendleton Inn, ladies and gentlemen. Meals at all hours. Running water— only you do the running. Entertainment for man and beast."

"But, dear child, that would be an imposition—"

"Then camp by the roadside," cried Pollyanna. "I've lived here a year, and I've never seen an excuse for an inn within forty miles. But we've got plenty to eat, and lots of room. This whole porch can be filled with cots, you know, so we can accommodate an army."

Tacitly accepting this hospitable invitation, they all alighted. Pollyanna was anxious to prepare a meal at once, but they insisted they had had luncheon, and were not at all hungry. And then Mr. Pendleton said casually, "By the way, Pollyanna, is your friend Luke very far from here?"

Pollyanna looked up at him. "Not so very far," she said breathlessly. "Why?"

"I've been telling Dr. Davies about him. The doctor's something of a specialist along those lines, and he'd like to look that boy over."

Pollyanna rose to her feet. "Aunt Ruth needs a nap," she announced. "We'll leave her here and go right over to Luke's."

Everyone laughed, and Aunt Ruth pretended to be deeply hurt by Pollyanna's willingness to desert her the moment she entered her home. But so absorbed was Pollyanna in the thoughts suggested by Uncle John's query, that Aunt Ruth's mock reproaches passed harmlessly over her head.

"I'll leave a note in the kitchen, Aunt Ruth, telling them you're here. You'd better sleep awhile."

"Much *I* matter," Aunt Ruth grumbled, but Pollyanna was rushing for her hat, and her relative laughed good-naturedly and gave her up.

Luke Geist and Mattie Murray were studying a lesson in geography, when John Pendleton's big car drove into the yard. Pollyanna went in to prepare Luke for visitors, and her heart was thumping.

Luke waved his hand gaily. "Mrs. Pendleton, if you were going to take a trip from Salt Lake City to Buffalo, New York, what roads would you take, what states would you pass through, and what—"

"Oh, don't expose my ignorance, Luke." Pollyanna's voice had an unnatural quality, as she herself noticed, and she saw that Luke looked up at her sharply. "I've brought you some visitors."

"All right. I like company. Who are they?"

"My uncle, Mr. Pendleton, is one. The other is Dr. Davies from Boston."

"A doctor?" Luke repeated. His face had gone white.

"He's a famous man, Luke, so my uncle says. He wants to look you over. He—he might be able to help you. Shall I bring him in?"

Luke closed his eyes. For a moment Pollyanna reproached herself for her lack of tact, and then wondered how it would be possible to make such a suggestion to an invalid without shocking his nerves. But in a moment, Luke looked up at her, and she saw that though he was colorless, even to his lips, he was master of himself. "Go ahead," he directed. "Bring 'em in."

"Very well. You come with me, Mattie." As the girl followed her out of the room, Pollyanna put an arm about her waist. "Mattie," she whispered,

"I feel as if something wonderful is going to happen."

There was a bench in the yard, on which Mrs. Geist placed her wash-tubs during the warm weather, and as, for a wonder, she was not washing today, Pollyanna and Mattie occupied the bench, and talked in lowered voices.

"Oh, Mrs. Pendleton," Mattie would whisper, clutching her friend's arm so tightly that it hurt. "Do you think—*do* you think they could help him?"

"I don't know, Mattie. We'll have to wait till the doctor has made his examination."

"Luke's been so brave when he thought he wasn't ever going to get better," Mattie went on. "I don't know how he'll feel if he finds out he has a chance."

"One thing I'm sure of," said Pollyanna. "He'll remember the friends who have stood by him in his helplessness." She noticed, with satisfaction, the color coming back to Mattie's white face.

John Pendleton appeared after what seemed a long time, and catching sight of the two, he came toward them. "Room for one more?"

"Plenty of room," said Pollyanna. "But I warn you it's for wash-tubs and not designed for tailor-made trousers like yours." Some instinct prompted her to keep him from speaking. She did not know how she could endure an unfavorable report.

Mr. Pendleton sat down beside her, and took her hand. "Pollyanna, Dr. Davies says your friend has not only a chance, but a mighty good one."

"Oh, Uncle John!" Pollyanna found that her eyes were streaming with tears. She leaned against his shoulder and managed to sob, "I don't know what ails me."

"I know, child. Waiting for a doctor's verdict in a case like this is waiting for a potential death-sentence. And now I'll tell you what the doctor wants to do. There is a very good hospital in Denver, and a surgeon in the city who is one of Dr. Davies' intimate friends. There's a train from your nearest railway point at ten o'clock to-night, and he wants to take Luke up with him."

"To-night?"

"Well, the sooner the better. Of course we'll have to interview the young man's parents. I imagine it will be easy to get their permission."

Pollyanna felt a sudden qualm. "You know, Uncle John, they haven't any money."

He patted her knee. "They won't need money. All we want is their permission."

Pollyanna snatched his hand and kissed it, and then jumped to her feet. "Mattie, do you know where Mrs. Geist hides herself when anyone comes? Get her as quickly as you can, and find from her where Mr. Geist is. After you've brought Mrs. Geist, go for him. If you need the car, take it."

Though Pollyanna had never seen Mr. Geist, she felt sure he must be a better dependence in a crisis than his wife. And as a matter of fact, when Luke's mother was brought weeping from her mysterious retreat, the only reply she made to question after question, was a feeble, "I don't know *what* to say."

"But Mrs. Geist," Pollyanna remonstrated, "if there's a chance for Luke to get better, you want him to take it, don't you?"

"I don't know *what* to say," cried the distracted woman, wringing her hands.

"Then I'll tell you what to say!" exclaimed Pollyanna. "Say, 'Yes, and God be thanked.'"

Mrs. Geist did not adopt this suggestion. "He hasn't got no clothes," she whimpered.

"Who? Oh, Luke, you mean. I hadn't got as far as clothes. What does he really own?"

"Just one pair of pajamas, besides what he's got on. His father wore his clothes out. What was the use in 'em hanging 'round, and bein' et up by moths?"

"Of course, Mrs. Geist. He can have some of my husband's things. Here are Mr. Geist and Mattie."

As she shook hands with Luke's father, she realized thankfully that he was more amenable to reason than his wife. It was evident at once that Mattie had explained the situation, for his first words were of gratitude.

"Mrs. Pendleton, you've been a good friend to us ever since you set foot in this house, but this here what Mattie's been telling me about means more than all the rest."

"You mustn't thank me, Mr. Geist. I want you to meet my uncle, Mr. Pendleton. You see we couldn't pick Luke up and carry him off without asking permission."

"Well, if it's permission you want, ma'am, you have it and a God bless you along with it. It does a man good to know that there's folks like you in the world."

Pollyanna had not seen Luke since the interview with the doctor. She went to his room now, and found an uncontrollable lump in her throat at the sight of his illumined face. Luke's eyes were red and swollen. It was clear that violent weeping had been the prelude to this radiant serenity.

She began to talk rapidly as a safeguard against tears. "Luke, I'm going to get together a few things of Mr. Pendleton's, so you will be ready for the journey. You see we didn't any of us know that you were going traveling so soon. You don't think he's too tired to undertake the trip to-night, do you, Dr. Davies?" she went on, turning to the doctor. "He could go to-morrow evening. Twenty-four hours won't make any difference, will they?"

Luke uttered a terrible cry. Pollyanna turned, aghast, thinking he must be in mortal pain, and never for a moment associating what she had just said with that cry of anguish. But Luke's eyes, just now suffused with tranquil light, were as fierce as a captured lion's.

"I'm going to-night," Luke burst out. "If there ain't no clothes for me, I'll wrap myself in sacking, but I'm going. Twenty-four hours lost don't make no difference, don't they? Wait till you've laid on your back five years, two months and twenty-eight days. Then you'll know better. Then you'll know that every hour matters, yes, and every minute, too."

"Gently, old man," said the doctor, putting his hand on the young fellow's shoulder. "Mrs. Pendleton didn't think, that's all. And we start to-night without fail."

There were tears in Pollyanna's eyes. "Yes, Luke, I didn't think," she said. "And I beg your pardon. Now, Luke, I'm going to take the doctor and my uncle back to my house for dinner, but they'll be here in plenty of time to get you ready. I won't see you till you come back so good-by and good luck."

She stooped and kissed him, and as she straightened up, Luke caught her hand. "Listen, Doc," he said huskily. "If you can do for me what you think you can, I'll owe you more than any man alive. But Mrs. Pendleton comes first. When she came I hated everybody. I felt the way a wolf does when he's in a trap, and gnaws off his leg, only gnawing off my leg wouldn't help none. But somehow or other, single-handed she pulled me out of hell, and whatever happens to me, it can't be as bad as it was."

The plan, as Pollyanna had learned it piecemeal, was for Uncle John and Aunt Ruth to stay with her for a week, while Dr. Davies remained in Denver, visiting his surgeon friend and doing what he could for Luke. At the end of a week, the Pendletons would drive to Denver, pick him up and go on to California. The surgeon insisted that he would have no trouble in getting Luke to the station in the big Packard, and an ambulance would meet the train in Denver. In order that they should have plenty of time to get Luke ready, Pollyanna hurried dinner somewhat, but she found a chance to pack a suitcase with the things Luke was likely to need.

At the dinner table, she thought it well to prepare Jimmy's mind for some surprises. "Jimmy, you mustn't expect to wear that grey suit again."

"What grey suit?" Jimmy demanded suspiciously.

"Why, the one that is getting tight for you. I'm sure you fussed enough about it the last time you wore it."

"Well, I suppose I can spare it," Jimmy said resignedly. "It's a pretty good suit, just the same."

"And you'll have to put up with being short on handkerchiefs and underwear, till an order can go to the place where you bought those last shirts, and back again. Pajamas are the worst of all. You have only one suit, besides the one you're wearing."

"Upon my word," Jimmy cried, looking around the table. "I believe the woman is confessing to grand larceny." But as he immediately urged her to have another slice of beef, it was plain he didn't hold her crime against her.

It had been decided that Jimmy should accompany the doctor to Luke's home, both because he was better able than Uncle John to help in the necessary lifting, and because he could easily direct the chauffeur to the station twenty miles distant. Indeed, it was to Jimmy that Pollyanna entrusted a heavy suitcase and he obediently placed it in the car, even though he looked hard at her and shook his head.

It was eleven o'clock before the car rolled into the yard again, and when Jimmy appeared he brought Mark in with him. The chauffeur evidently felt a little shy over meeting his employers in a social way, and sat as far from them as possible. Clifford Wright had joined the company since Jimmy's departure, and he explained hurriedly that he had only been waiting to hear how Luke had stood the ride to the train.

"Fine, just fine!" declared Jimmy, poking up the fire. "But I hope nobody's going to leave yet awhile, for I haven't had a chance to do any talking, and it isn't every day we have visitors from Boston."

"Well, Jimmy!" exclaimed Aunt Ruth, "I certainly am glad I came. For a full year I've been worried about Pollyanna, but I must say, I never saw her looking better."

Pollyanna pulled her chair closer to her husband's, and slipped her hand into his. "We're glad, too, we came, aren't we, dear?"

"We certainly are," Jimmy said emphatically. "This job's been the turning-point with me, Aunt Ruth, nothing can stop me now."

"I don't like to be a mere echo," said Dorothy, "but *I'm* glad I came." Her significant glance just brushed her lover, but Clifford betrayed her by turning a deep, painful and yet ecstatic crimson.

"And *I'm* glad I came," cried Pollyanna, "for a million reasons. It isn't only because Jimmy's done so splendidly in his work, but just think of Luke

Geist. Of course it's all Uncle John's generosity, just as my library is mostly Aunt Ruth's generosity, but how glad I am that I came here and found Luke so Uncle John could help him."

"And I'm glad *I* came," said Uncle John, giving her back her smile. "It's worth a longer trip than this just to find that a year in the West hasn't changed our Pollyanna."

THE END